"Callum, what was his name?"

He broke every rule in the book, hoping to make Molly feel better. Instead, he made it worse, saying, "Arthur Jay Killian."

She drew a shaky breath. "Oh my God."

"Molly? Do you know him?"

"I was instrumental in putting him in prison."

"Molly, what happened? With this Killian guy."

She swallowed and tightened her lips, then spoke. "He was a vicious man. Unbelievably vicious. What he did to his wife? It was almost as bad as what he did to the women here. But he did it to her more than once."

"Why isn't he after his wife?" Callum asked.

"I guess she got as far away under a new name as I'd hoped."

"Which leaves you."

"That would be my guess. But why the other women? Why didn't he just come after *me*?"

"You'll have to ask *him* that when we cuff him."

CONARD COUNTY: CHRISTMAS CRIME SPREE

New York Times Bestselling Author

RACHEL LEE

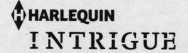

HARLEQUIN

INTRIGUE

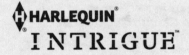

ISBN-13: 978-1-335-58222-5

Conard County: Christmas Crime Spree

Copyright © 2022 by Susan Civil-Brown

Harlequin Enterprises ULC
22 Adelaide St. West, 41st Floor
Toronto, Ontario M5H 4E3, Canada
www.Harlequin.com

Printed in U.S.A.

Recycling programs
for this product may
not exist in your area.

Rachel Lee was hooked on writing by the age of twelve and practiced her craft as she moved from place to place all over the United States. This *New York Times* bestselling author now resides in Florida and has the joy of writing full-time.

Books by Rachel Lee

Harlequin Intrigue

Conard County: The Next Generation

Cornered in Conard County
Missing in Conard County
Murdered in Conard County
Conard County Justice
Conard County: Hard Proof
Conard County: Traces of Murder
Conard County: Christmas Bodyguard
Conard County: Mistaken Identity
Conard County: Christmas Crime Spree

Visit the Author Profile page at Harlequin.com.

CAST OF CHARACTERS

Molly Canton—Pastor of Good Shepherd Church, faces difficulties because of her gender. Naturally cheerful and generous.

Detective Callum McCloud—Widower, new to Conard County, moved from Boston where he was a detective. Seeking quieter life.

Tyra Lansing—Molly's best friend, victim of brutal home invasion.

Callisto Manx—A church warden and Molly's ally.

Arthur Killian—Seeks vengeance against Molly. He doesn't care who he hurts to make her suffer.

Chapter One

Reverend Molly Canton, pastor of Good Shepherd Church in Conard City, Wyoming, saw gently falling snow outside her study window. The snowflakes sparkled in the light gleaming from her window.

Enchanted, she rose, slipped into her red parka and stepped outside to enjoy a miracle of the Christmas season.

The cold nipped at her cheeks as she looked upward into the darkened night sky, but she hardly felt it. All that this perfection needed, she thought, was quiet Christmas carols in the background. With an inward giggle, she stuck out her tongue like a kid to catch a drifting flake.

To think, she would have missed this beauty if insomnia hadn't plagued her tonight. Snow floating down like this in the daytime carried little of the magic of lightly falling snow at night.

Turning, she looked up at the glowing steeple of the church, a soft light, meant to be a beacon to the faithful but faded a bit in the fog of the falling snow.

Her heart soared with the rising steeple, lifting toward the heavens.

Cares and concerns vanished in the moment, making her feel as free as that shimmering snow. Almost as if she fell upward into it. Joy, never far from her at this time of year, flooded her now. Gratitude filled her.

She began to shiver and accepted the fact that she'd have to go back indoors, when she heard a sound.

It immediately caught her attention. Had it been a cry of some kind? Certainly not a baby; she'd recognize that sound. Did someone need help? Turning slowly, she strained her ears and held her breath as much as she could. The foggy clouds that had been issuing from her mouth and nose subsided to almost nothing.

Maybe she'd imagined it? Probably. Being alone in the near dark often stimulated the imagination. And she was certainly imaginative.

But just as she had decided she'd heard nothing at all, she heard the cry again. Someone *was* in trouble. A woman.

Her joy dropped away, replaced by a need for action. Adrenaline began to course through her, making her skin prickle. But where had the cry come from? Was it really distress? She pulled back her hood, hoping to hear better.

Near the church like this, sounds could echo off the high stone walls. At the same time, the increasing depth of the winter's snow muffled the world.

Unable to ignore the call, needing to place it, she stepped away from her parsonage and continued along the walkway to the church that a member of her congregation kept clear for her. Tonight it was lightly dusted with fresh snow between the banks of previous snows. Maybe standing somewhere else would localize the sound…if it came again.

That had sounded like a cry of distress, though. Not simply an exclamation. If someone was hurt, she had to find them. Quickly. The lack of sirens indicated no one had called 911. She must be alone—the woman who had cried out.

Urgency filled Molly. Her pace quickened, her snow boots squeaking quietly on the wet pavement. The nights in this town were so quiet in the wee hours. There was no sound except trucks whizzing by on the state highway bypass.

She heard the cry again. From the far side of the church. She ran around the building, hoping she could find it. Then she saw a dim light in the upstairs bedroom of the house on the other side of the large churchyard.

Mabel Blix. A woman in her early thirties who lived alone, confined now to crutches and sometimes a wheelchair because of an auto accident.

Molly wasted no time running to Mabel's door. It was unlocked, so she raced inside, past family heirlooms, and charged up the stairs.

What she found made her pull out her cell phone and call the cops and the ambulance.

Mabel sprawled on the floor and she looked as if she had been beaten. Molly knelt beside her, calling her name, letting her know she was not alone. That help was on the way.

DETECTIVE CALLUM MCCLOUD arrived at the crime scene, dragged out of the most restful sleep he'd had in a while. Not that he hadn't once been used to these calls, but he'd hoped to find far fewer in this little out-of-the-way place. Now here he was in the thick of it again.

The crime-scene tape had already been strung around the house and environs. A small crowd had begun to collect despite the early hour, but no more than the county deputies and local police could hold easily at bay. From voices around him, he gathered that most of these people had known the victim. Small town, he reminded himself.

Crime-scene techs were already at work, bright lights flooded the yard and every light in the house had been turned on. As Callum reached the edge of the tape, one of the techs handed him a folded-up clean suit, gloves and booties to prevent contamination of the scene. He pulled them on, then yanked up the hood, tightening it with the drawstrings. Only then did he cross the barrier.

A path had been neatly delineated, with yellow tape laid on either side, indicating the areas the crime-scene team had already cleared. He stuck within those lines as he approached the front porch of the small two-story house. It was a routine entirely too familiar to him. Sickeningly familiar.

The pathway had been marked, up and into the

house, where techs were busy at work. Floodlights glared over everything. Some of the team nodded briefly his way as he entered the home, and the lead technician approached.

"We cleared the stairs and the bedroom upstairs. You can go up if you want."

He definitely did. These hours after the home invasion could be the most important. "The victim?"

"Barely conscious. Blow to the head. She won't be able to tell you much right away."

Callum nodded, glancing around as flash cameras recorded every detail. Home invasion? Maybe. Objects had been smashed and thrown around. Items trampled.

But the biggest puzzle of all: a large-screen TV hanging from the wall. So what had the perp been seeking? Money in a rolled-up sock? Jewels that were probably mostly paste with the possible exception of an heirloom or two?

This didn't look right to his practiced eye.

He made his way into the bedroom and found more wanton destruction. Drawers pulled open or dumped, clothing thrown about. A jewelry box that appeared to have been shaken upside down. A few cheap pieces left behind. How did the perp know the difference, if there was one?

Blood on the pale blue rug, but not a dangerous amount.

Something nagged at him. He'd need to talk to the victim, study the crime-scene photos in detail. Well, that was standard procedure, but this time he felt there was something more he needed to figure out.

Returning outside, he asked the deputy who was standing just outside the door, Guy Redwing, "Who found the victim?"

"The pastor did."

Immediately, Callum scanned the crowd, searching among the men for a clerical collar. "The pastor?" he repeated.

Redwing pointed. "She's standing right there in the red parka."

She. Well, he hadn't expected that, not around here. Big cities were one thing, and they often still had trouble with female clerics. But a small area like this? It was also a sign of how little he'd come to know this community in the last few months.

There she stood, wrapped in her red parka, her hands stuffed in her pockets, her fur-lined hood pulled up but not tightened around her face. Jeans. Winter boots.

Bucking the image, he thought with dry amusement.

"Molly Canton," the deputy advised him. "Some call her 'Reverend,' most call her 'Pastor' and some call her names I won't repeat. Two years ain't long enough to change some attitudes around here."

Callum dragged up one corner of his mouth. "You got that right, Guy. Or anywhere."

He quickly stripped off his protective gear and tossed it toward one of the crime scene crew, then headed to the pastor.

The crowd of lookie-loos had been growing steadily since he entered the house. Molly Canton wasn't being eased away from the tape, however. Her face reflected deep concern, and she didn't back away from him, but held out her gloved hand. He shook it.

"I'm Detective Callum McCloud, and you're Reverend Canton, right?"

"I am. I've seen you around a couple of times, Detective. I wish we'd met under better circumstances." At least she hadn't pressed him to join her flock.

"I'd like to have a few words with you, if you don't mind."

"I don't mind."

"Not out here, ma'am. Too many ears."

She nodded. "Come around to my cottage and I'll make coffee, or tea if you prefer."

He followed her along the shoveled walkway to the rear of the church. *Cottage* was a good name for it, he supposed. Maybe *cozy* in some people's parlance. Half the small stone house boasted a second floor that looked like a square tower, a single large room by itself. Unlike the rest of the cottage, it was covered in gray clapboard.

Inside the house was warm enough, but the rooms were small.

"I've often wondered how any of my predecessors could have raised a family in here," Molly remarked as she set about starting the coffee. "You a tea man?"

"Coffee for me."

"Easier." Then, as it began brewing, she doffed her parka and they sat down across from each other at a wooden table. "Any word on Mabel? The victim?"

"I'm told she's groggy. We won't be able to talk to her for at least a few hours."

"I'm so glad I found her alive." Molly's gentle face sagged.

Indeterminate age, Callum thought. Silver streaks in her dark hair. A bit plump around the middle, he'd noticed when she shed her jacket. She wore a pair of metal-rimmed glasses, "half-eyes" as they'd once been called. Middle-aged, maybe? Not to judge by her youthful face, a soft, pretty oval with a delicate nose. Curiosity pricked him.

"So you found Ms. Blix? How did that happen? Exactly."

"I was working in my study."

"At this hour?"

She gave him a crooked smile that wrinkled her nose just a tiny bit. "I'm sometimes an insomniac. This was one of those nights. Anyway, the light from my window caught a gentle snowfall, and it was just too beautiful to ignore. So I went outside to enjoy it. A little Christmas miracle."

He felt his face stiffen and hoped it didn't show. Miracles? He didn't believe in them, not the smallest of them.

Molly got up and poured their coffee, then leaned back against the counter to sip. "Regardless, I was enjoying the snow. This is my favorite time of year, and this was a touch of magic. For me, anyway. Then I thought I heard a cry. I wasn't sure, though. Then it came again and there was no mistaking it was a woman. She sounded in pain."

He nodded, pulled out his pocket notebook and scribbled some notes in it.

"Well, it's hard to tell where sounds come from, especially at night, when they can carry so far. I moved, hoping a different position would help. The stone walls of this church are famous for echoing."

He wrote some more.

"I came around the corner to the front of the church, and saw that Mabel's bedroom light was on which doesn't mean anything by itself. She was in a terrible car accident that left her needing crutches. The light usually stays on in case she needs to go to the bathroom. But I heard the cry again and knew it had to be her."

Molly paused to sip coffee and clearly collect herself. "I thought maybe she'd fallen and couldn't get up. I hurried over and the door was unlocked, so I charged in. I didn't much notice the mess downstairs I was in such a hurry. Then I found Mabel. It was obvious she'd been beaten. I gave what first aid I could until the ambulance arrived." Molly's face sagged.

"I noticed the mess when I was with Molly, then when I came downstairs." She looked directly at Callum. "It was a robbery, wasn't it? Although I can't think Mabel had a thing to steal."

"Jewelry?" Callum asked.

Molly shook her head. "She only had a couple of good pieces, heirlooms, and they weren't big enough to sell for much. Mostly sentimental value. Like a lot of people in this town, she was hanging by a financial thread, even talking about selling some of her antiques."

Callum nodded slowly and at last sipped some coffee. "Nobody who might have a problem with her?"

Molly shook her head. "Only the drunk who rammed into her car, and he's in jail right now. Although how he could blame *her*..." Molly frowned.

"You know her well?"

"She's a member of my congregation. I check in on her often, as do some of the other ladies. Being on crutches and in a wheelchair makes her life difficult. She hasn't had time to adjust to any of it yet. And I hope she never has to."

Callum nodded his agreement. But now, especially with a blow to the head, things might well grow more difficult for Mabel Blix.

He drained his coffee. "Thank you, Pastor. I may be in touch with more questions."

"No problem," she replied. "Often enough you'll have to drag me out of the middle of something, though."

"Busy?"

"The territory of this calling. Anyway, I'll be going to the hospital soon."

He hesitated as he reached for his jacket. "We don't want Ms. Blix's memory affected."

She screwed up her face. "Polluted, you mean. Well, I'm not going for any reason but to offer her comfort. And believe me, Detective McCloud, nobody will keep Mabel's pastor away."

WHAT A DOUR MAN, Molly thought as she changed into clerical garb. Black slacks in deference to the cold, black lace-up boots with respect to the snow and a long-sleeved black clerical shirt with plastic collar stuck in beneath the shirt tabs.

She hated that plastic collar—she preferred cotton—but the expense of keeping cotton pristine and starched had changed her thinking. She could keep plastic clean with an all-purpose cleaner. Didn't mean she had to like it.

Finally, she donned a dark gray wool coat and a scarf that could be pulled up over her head. Official-looking. The way people expected her to look, unlike the red parka she wore when the cold was brutal enough. Her own version of kicking over the traces.

But after nearly two years of working to win this county over to the idea of a female pastor, she wasn't about to blow it now. That task was far from completed. Her red parka might get a wink and a nudge, but it would have been foolish for her to go beyond that.

She thought of Detective Callum McCloud as she drove toward the hospital at the edge of town. His was not likely to be a face that Mabel would want to see on waking. Lord, how could a man look so unrelievedly grim? Tall, lanky but…grim. She'd seen him around a few times and was quite sure she'd never seen him smile.

But he was not her concern. Mabel was, and even if they weren't allowing friends to visit her yet, Molly could walk through those same doors as if they didn't exist.

She parked in a space reserved for clergy, although

there weren't many of them around here, and entered the hospital. Here again, she knew most everyone by sight if not by name and they knew her. The advantage of being a pastor of the largest church in a small town. She would never be invisible.

But maybe that could be a disadvantage, too, she thought with a slight grimace. Not that she'd yet found a reason for it to be.

She was taken to Mabel's room without a problem, only to be told she'd have to wait. Mabel had gone to surgery for bleeding on the brain.

Molly didn't need a doctor to explain th danger to her. She'd seen it during her time in the National Guard. She folded her hands, closed her eyes and began a heartfelt prayer for Mabel Blix. The poor woman had suffered more than enough.

MIDMORNING, MABEL RETURNED to her room in a medically induced coma and the doctors had no idea when she might waken.

Molly left, truly distressed for Mabel, and headed back to the parsonage because she had other duties that required her attention. She claimed very little of her days solely for herself, which was fine by her. She'd always felt that busy was best.

There was a lunch that day at the bakery for the ladies who devoted so much time to keeping the church in excellent shape. They called themselves the Altar Society, and were a group of ten who managed busy lives in addition to helping out at the church with everything from cleaning to darning linens when they needed it.

The lunch was always an enjoyable experience, but so was the tea these same women presented monthly for other volunteers, such as ushers. A good group to share time with.

Today, however, the robbery of Mabel Blix was the subject of all conversation. They'd gathered in a small room reserved by Melinda, who owned the bakery, for group meetings. The pastries were hell on Molly's perennial diet.

"Surely you know something about last night, Pastor," Janice Remy remarked. She was an older woman with perfectly coiffed hair and a penchant for flowered dresses. She chaired the Altar Society and was often the most outspoken of the group. She was also the leading gossip in that she managed to ferret out the details of nearly everything that happened around here and wasn't shy about sharing them. It was a good thing she was not mean-spirited.

Nine other faces silently asked the same question. Molly debated how much she could share without crossing lines of confidentiality—lines she guarded stringently. She settled on the simplest answer.

"Just about Mabel. She needed some surgery and won't be awake for some time yet. No visitors. I'll check in this afternoon."

Claire AuCoin spoke. A gray-haired woman in her elder years, it hardly mattered that Janice was the titular head of the group. Claire had been serving so many years in the society that she was the de facto leader. It always amused Molly how any group, however small, had lines of authority.

Nor did Claire bow to formalities. For her, a patterned Western shirt and jeans were fine for anything except Sunday services.

"Tell Mabel we'll start a prayer circle for her," Claire said. "That woman has been through more than enough. I can't believe this has happened!"

The subtext being that crimes like this were rare in this city and county. Perhaps. But who knew what went on behind closed doors?

Janice took charge again. "The linens need dry cleaning again and, Georgia, I thought I saw some frayed edges that need mending."

Georgia, mender and darner par excellence, nodded her dark head. "I thought it was getting to be about time again." She was a woman with great skill, but was seriously overweight and always trying to hide the fact behind loose, flowy garments in dark colors. Molly thought of it as style.

The conversation moved on to lighter subjects, away from the church. Who was expecting a baby, how youngsters were getting along in school. The snowmen that were springing up in the city park. Whether the city's ice-skating rink, a depression filled with water every winter, was growing hard enough for the children to break out their skates, or the boys to bring out their hockey sticks and pucks. The general agreement was that the ice must be safe by now.

After the luncheon, Molly made two home visits,

one to a dear woman in the last stages of breast cancer, Stacy Withers, who always said, "The mammogram didn't catch it."

Why this was so important to Stacy, Molly had no
idea, and she didn't ask. She suspected that Stacy felt
betrayed by medical science, but medical science had
kept her going this long, and was now easing the pain
of her last months. Molly's rule was never to pry unless a person said something that seemed to invite it.

This time, however, Stacy had something to add.
"It happened too fast, Pastor. Too fast. Once a year
for a mammogram wasn't often enough for me. Not
nearly."

Molly took her hand. "Are you feeling you should
have done more?" She hated to think that Stacy might
in some way be feeling guilty about her illness. She
already felt guilty about leaving her family behind.

"I guess I couldn't have," Stacy said after a few
moments. "But I feel so betrayed. My family feels
betrayed."

"Because you got sick?"

Stacy gave her a hollow-eyed look. "How can God
do this to my children?"

A question with no decent answer, Molly thought
sadly as she drove away. The usual bromides were
useless. Certainly useless to Stacy.

Her next visit was to a man who worked hard at
being a crusty curmudgeon from the confines of his
recliner and wheelchair. He could have been amusing

except that he took out most of his bad temper on his daughter, who looked ragged from caring for him.

"Get some help," Molly told her.

Marcia Lathrop just gave her an exhausted look. "My brother lives too far away."

"Not so far he can't get over here for a weekend. And I bet he could pay for some home care to give you a break once in a while."

Marcia simply shook her head.

"I can get some folks over here to give you a few hours from time to time."

Again, Marcia shook her head. "I can do this."

Molly decided to see how many volunteers she could rustle up to help Marcia, anyway. Enough of this, she thought with annoyance. She doubted anyone in her fold had the least idea that Marcia was handling this all alone. Marcia never, ever complained. Too bad if she didn't want to accept "charity" from the church. There was a point when independence reached self-immolation.

She swung by the hospital to check on Mabel Blix and ran in to Callum McCloud on his way out. She paused to greet him and he simply shook his head.

"She's still out, Pastor. The doc told me another day at least. I've called her family and they're flying in from Seattle. And before you think you should have done that, let me remind you that delivering the bad news when there's a crime is *my* job."

Molly studied the dour man and wondered how

many times he'd had to face that hell, often in worse circumstances than this. "Thank you," she said finally.

For once, a corner of his mouth lifted. "Do I detect guilt? Don't bother. The family will need your services more when they arrive tomorrow."

Molly watched him walk away into snow that had begun to fall heavily, then she headed back to the church. It was still the Christmas season, and one of her favorite things awaited her: after-school care.

Nearly thirty children, aged five to ten, crowded the church basement. Their high, piping voices shared the excitement they all felt as they worked on various projects. Some were stringing popcorn and others gluing together construction-paper rings, all to make garlands for their trees at home. A few concentrated with creased brows as they tried to make papier-mâché angels. Some painted small plaster images of bells, baubles and Santa Clauses. A few had brought in their school photos to make more personalized items.

Their excitement was infectious, and soon Molly shed the earlier part of the day to join them around their small tables and admire their artwork.

Laura Maskin, the retired teacher in charge, never stopped moving around the room, dispensing encouraging words. Her helper, Belinda Armistead, did the same.

It was beautiful, controlled chaos, and this excitement was part of what Molly loved so much about this season. These kids could barely contain themselves as Christmas drew nearer. Their cheer infused Molly.

She was sorry to see the children leave as their parents arrived to pick them up.

But after she helped clean up the church basement, the evening would be hers. This town, for whatever reason, didn't lend itself to evening prayers. She was often lucky to get a handful of people on weekday mornings. But Sundays made up for all that.

She decided to make one last swing through the church, then head back to her cottage for a bowl of hot soup and a good thriller. Her secret vice, those thrillers. Although she didn't know how secret it could be when they were stuffed on her bookshelf below all the religious texts. Anyone who came in would be bound to see them.

The hardest part of her current position was having to follow the straight and narrow so carefully. Moving here hadn't been easy, not when she found herself regarded with so much suspicion and sexism. Women shouldn't be pastors, evidently.

But that had been wearing off, and her biggest success to date had been suggesting they dress the figures in the crèche as the poor people they likely had been. Donations of tattered clothing had poured in, and the congregation had taken great pleasure in dressing the figures.

But it somehow seemed right in a county where so many people were living on a ragged economic edge. She guessed a lot of people must have felt the same.

It also struck her that the Wise Men, who hadn't been present at the birth and hadn't shown up for two years, shouldn't be out there garbed in finery and bearing expensive gifts that had done the Holy Family little enough good.

Her personal rebellion.

With soup warm in her tummy, she grabbed a well-thumbed paperback and was about to dive in when she remembered that the Vestry was meeting in the morning.

That was *not* a joyous part of this season, or any season. They had hired her, but all she ever heard was a litany of how the church could be doing better, what oversights they deemed her guilty of and a bunch of other unpleasantries.

Oh, well. It came with the position.

But instead of reading, or thinking about the wardens, her thoughts turned to Detective Callum Mc-Cloud. Dour and grim, yes, but there was a story behind that disposition somewhere. A sad or ugly one. Someone with his experience and background didn't just choose an out-of-the-way place like this.

He was running from something, she decided. Hiding from it. Escaping it.

But he would have been one heck of a handsome man if he'd ever smiled. She'd caught just a glimpse of it that afternoon outside the hospital.

Well, maybe she could thaw him a bit with a touch of Christmas spirit. And tomorrow, she simply had to get that artificial tree out of the attic and set it up down here.

Bringing the season indoors was part of the joy. Twinkling lights, happy kids and mostly smiling parents.

Definitely the best time of year.

CALLUM MCCLOUD'S THOUGHTS drifted to Molly Canton as he sat in his rented house, with its ragged furniture, and sipped a bourbon. He'd sensed steel in her, a tensile strength that probably stood her in good stead even as she nurtured her flock.

That remark she made about how no one would keep the pastor away from Mabel Blix had included the subtext that not even he, a detective, could keep her away. The woman might bend some when she judged it necessary, but he doubted she ever broke.

He'd seen enough of her to know how pretty she was. That probably didn't help her cause any, although the streaks of early gray probably did.

In front of him, on a battered coffee table, he'd spread out the reports he had about the Blix attack. Neighbor interviews. Scene photos.

And nothing fit. During his long career, he'd seen enough home invasions to know when one was a burglary. This hadn't been. This kind of attack was something he'd only seen when the perp had a personal grudge.

But to hear the neighbors tell it, no one disliked her. She had a great many friends, and no current romantic relationship. She didn't even have an ex lingering in her background somewhere. No, she'd spent her entire young life here in this town and had lately worked as a recorder in the county's property office. Nothing in her job should have drawn this kind of ire.

Hell, he hated cases like this. Cases without an avenue to pursue. Cases that didn't yield immediate clues. Not one thing to hang his hat on.

He rose and went to refresh his bourbon, reminding himself it had to be his last. Drinking too much after his wife's death hadn't helped anything, but it had brought him close to some serious trouble. Angela would have hated that.

But he'd tried to leave Angela behind him, taking nothing with him when he left Boston except photo albums. No furniture, no mementos, no other reminders. And thus, he had brought himself to this one-horse town that shouldn't remind him of anything.

Until early this morning, anyway.

Cussing loudly because he didn't have to be quiet about it while he was alone like this, he went back to the coffee table and stood over it, wondering if a fan could blow all that paper and those photographs into something meaningful.

All too often, though, there *was* no meaning, as he knew from personal experience. Finding meaning in the violence of this world was like Diogenes searching for an honest man.

The only real meaning Callum had been able to find was that humans were brutes. Much of the time they kept it under control, but sometimes it burst out and it didn't need a meaning.

It might have a reason, but never a meaning. And most of the reasons were so half-baked they hardly bore repeating.

He passed a hand over his eyes, knowing full well that he wasn't going to find a clue or an answer tonight. No way.

Then his cell phone rang. It was the dispatcher at the sheriff's department, Velma, she of the indeterminate age and smoke-roughened voice.

"Hey, Detective," she said politely enough. "Pastor Canton wants you to call her. Need the number?"

He supposed the church number was written in capital letters on any web search, but he asked for it, anyway. People always liked to feel useful.

And what the hell did Molly Canton want from him, anyway? His heart quickened a bit. Had she found some kind of clue?

He tapped in her number immediately.

"Molly Canton," she answered cheerfully. Not even a title.

"This is Detective McCloud," he replied. "You wanted me to call?"

"Yes. I know I'm being forward and you have every right to tell me to get lost, but I realized I need a tall man for a bit of help. And you're tall."

He was hardly a ladder, he thought. "What is it?"

"I'm trying to get my Christmas tree out of the attic and I can't quite reach it."

Christmas tree? For several seconds he felt stunned.

"I understand it's an imposition and if you say no, I won't be offended. I promise."

He glanced at the clock—9:30 p.m. And she wanted a Christmas tree out of her attic. He shook his head and opened his mouth to say something sharp, then different words escaped him.

"I'll be right over, Pastor."

Damn it, he thought as he disconnected and reached for his cold-weather gear. What had come over him?

A freaking Christmas tree.

Chapter Two

Callum arrived at the parsonage five minutes later. To his surprise, Molly Canton was standing outside, parka unzipped, staring up into heavily falling snow.

When she heard him, she looked at him with a huge smile. "Best time of the year, don't you think?"

Not really. But he kept the thought to himself. "Where's this tree?"

"In the attic, like I said. One of the church handymen put it away for me last year and now I can't reach it. I can't thank you enough for coming over. I made some hot cocoa to warm you up, though. One benefit of doing a favor for a neighbor."

Hot cocoa? He hadn't had any of that in years. He wondered how it would mix with the bourbon in his stomach.

"But don't let me keep you longer than necessary," she said briskly, turning toward the door. "I'm really awful for having brought you out at this time of night. But as my congregants can tell you, once I get an idea, I don't let go easily."

He took a shot in the dark as he followed her into the warmly lit interior. "Like the crèche out front?"

She laughed as she shed her parka. "Like that."

"I kind of like it," he admitted reluctantly.

"A surprising number of people do, which is probably why I still have this job."

He dropped his jacket over the back of one of her kitchen chairs, then followed her up narrow stairs.

"A house of another era," she remarked. "No wasted space. I guess that's why the furniture is darn near as old as the house. Hard to remove."

"A little demolition and some build-it-yourself furniture might solve that problem."

"Agh. And here I had a lazy reason for leaving everything as it is."

Callum suspected this woman was in no way lazy. Not in this job. Not wanting her Christmas tree at an hour when most people were flopped in front of a TV or in bed. "Anything else up in that attic that you might need?"

She glanced at him with a smile. "One trip only?"

"I didn't say that." But he'd probably meant it. He didn't want to become anyone's errand boy.

"I don't plan to keep imposing," she replied as she pointed out the trapdoor overhead. "At least a former resident put in drop-down stairs. Can you imagine trying to reach in there from a wobbly ladder?"

"I'd probably become a statistic."

At least there was a pull-string light above the stairs. It wasn't bright, but bright enough. "That long box?" he asked when he was up to his waist in the small space.

"Please."

This was going to be fun. Neither the trapdoor nor the drop-down stairs would be wide enough to simply pull the box out and slide it down beside him. He'd have to back down while pulling the box.

"How many guys put this up here?" he asked.

"Two," she answered. "Is it too much for you to handle?"

Like he'd ever admit to that. "Just a little more complicated. Stand away from the bottom of the stairs."

Then he reached for the box and began his perilous journey, dragging it with him as he backed down. He was halfway down when he had enough of a grip to pull it out all the way and lower it. Molly reached for it.

"Thank you so much!"

He could hear the smile in her voice. Damn woman was too nice. "Anything else before I pull out of here?"

"Well, there are two other boxes. One with ornaments and one with garlands."

"You packed the garlands separately?"

"I didn't want them to get crushed. Besides, it meant smaller boxes."

Thank God for that. The first box barely fit through the opening and he barked his knuckles a little, but no big deal. The second box was easier. "Anything else?" he asked again.

"I hate to impose…"

As if she already hadn't. "What? Just tell me."

"There's another two boxes. Outdoor decorations. But it's not necessary…"

He gave up and climbed into the enclosed space. "Good thing I'm not claustrophobic." Crouched in the small space, he found the other two boxes. This time he dumped them slowly through the opening. Molly caught them.

"I can't thank you enough," she told him warmly.

His mother had raised him to be a gentleman, although sometimes he wondered why she had bothered. "No problem," he answered.

He climbed down, raised the stairs, then brushed himself off. "Someone needs to get up there to dust before it becomes a fire hazard. And no, I'm *not* volunteering."

"I'd think you were out of your mind if you did." But her mossy green eyes twinkled at him. "You're a kind man."

That was open to debate. "Where do you want these?"

"Oh, I can move them into the living room. You've already done enough."

He smothered a sigh, the gentleman in him rising to the fore again. "I'll do it."

The living room was small, just a few chairs and a fireplace that looked as if it hadn't been used in quite a while. It was too damn clean.

When he'd placed all the boxes out of the way as best he could, he brushed his hands together.

Molly spoke. "Now for that hot cocoa I promised you."

"That's not necessary."

"It's already almost done. Come to the kitchen, Detective."

"Just Callum," he told her.

"Then I'm just Molly."

When he was seated at the small table, she placed a large, steaming cup of cocoa in front of him. He couldn't remember the last time he'd had any. When he'd been a kid?

He eyed her as she sat across from him. "Aren't you having any?"

"Too many calories."

He paused with the mug halfway to his mouth. "What?"

She waved a hand, still smiling. "I need to take off fifteen pounds or so."

"According to who? Hollywood? TV commercials?"

"I don't like looking motherly. Although maybe that helps in my current position."

Callum shook his head. "You look just fine." Then he tasted the cocoa and was relieved it didn't go to war with the bourbon he'd swallowed earlier. In fact, it tasted wonderful.

"Great cocoa," he said.

"I'm glad you like it."

When he emptied his cup, she poured him another from the pan on the stove.

"It was awfully nice of you to come out this late at night," she said.

He eyed her over the rim of his mug and told the truth. "I wasn't relaxing."

"Looking over the case?"

"I don't let go easily."

She sighed and rested her chin in her hand. "I can't believe anyone would do that to Mabel. It would be hard to find a sweeter soul. And that car accident. Well, I'm not a vengeful person by nature, but I'm glad the drunk driver is in jail. Such lack of consideration for the lives of others in order to indulge an addiction. Or a quest for brief pleasure."

He didn't disagree and buried his own guilty conscience. At least he'd always summoned a cab.

"Now this," Molly continued. "I simply cannot fathom why anyone would want to hurt her. And they *wanted* to hurt her, didn't they?"

He couldn't answer that question even though he believed she was right. "I can't discuss the case."

"To think of Mabel being a case." Molly shook her head, then said, "I'm not trying to pry. Just ruminating. And I shouldn't be reminding you of work."

"It's not easy to put aside. Don't apologize." She had a way about her, he thought. A nature that invited people to talk with her. He needed to be careful around her.

AFTER CALLUM LEFT, Molly stood in her living room surrounded by boxes she needed to unpack. Inviting Callum over to help get the items from the attic had been a brainstorm. She could have asked some of the men from church in the morning, but she'd thought of dour Callum, new in town, probably all alone.

It was the only way she could think of to get a chance to make him feel welcome.

But she'd been utterly surprised when he'd agreed. She hadn't expected that at all.

She flushed a bit when she thought of how difficult it had been for one man to handle those boxes. Hard enough for the guys last year to get them up there, but where else was she to put them?

Feeling not at all sleepy yet, and wondering if she faced another night of insomnia, she opened the box that contained the fiber-optic tree and placed the tree in the corner, in front of the bookcase and beside a small writing desk, the only place it would fit.

The tree had been left behind by her predecessor. It was an extravagance she never would have purchased herself, and the instant she plugged it in she felt the sparkle of magic once again. She went to her small CD player, popped in a disc of Christmas music and settled back into an overstuffed chair to let the beauty of the moments wash over her.

Decorating could wait for tomorrow. She'd probably need the enjoyment after meeting with the wardens.

At some point she drifted into sleep, "Silent Night" following her into her dreams.

For a little while, all was right with the world.

Chapter Three

All was right with the world until her meeting with the wardens. Sometimes she wanted to ask them outright why they'd hired her.

John Jason stepped onto his usual soapbox, bemoaning the fact that contributions had fallen off since Molly had taken over as pastor.

Daniel Alder wanted Molly to give a homily about the Christian duty to tithe to the church.

At that, Molly couldn't remain closemouthed. "Our primary duty is to help our fellow man," she said pleasantly. "There are a great many people in this county who need help. Regardless, my first responsibility is not to fill church coffers."

Silence greeted her. She was surprised only that no one erupted.

After a pregnant pause, John Jason spoke again. "This is the season of giving. Surely people can offer a little."

Callisto Manx, the only female member of the group, spoke. "Pastor Molly is supposed to be our spiritual guide, not our chief fundraiser."

John snorted. "Be that as it may, if the pastor wants to talk about helping our fellow man, at present there is no financial path to offering our annual Christmas baskets and the Christmas dinner."

Molly spoke again, disliking the way they were talking, as if she wasn't in the room. "I've spoken to the market. They're donating ten cooked turkeys for the dinner and a whole lot of canned ham for the baskets. Then, of course, we have the high school donating the use of their kitchen and cafeteria."

Silence fell again. John drummed his fingers on the long table. "Well, if you can do that, do more."

"I was thinking about asking our congregation to donate items for the baskets and for the dinner. A potluck sort of thing."

"That'll work," Callisto announced. "Some things are better than money, and folks feel better about giving them."

"The church has expenses," John reminded them with a glare in Molly's direction.

"And toys," Molly said, ignoring him. "A lot of children will need Christmas gifts. We need to put up the giving tree soon."

"And that still won't pay the light bill!"

"But candles will work." Molly smiled brightly. "Think how beautiful that would be."

When the meeting broke up in the early afternoon, Molly knew she was once again skating on thin ice. Nothing new about that, unfortunately.

She understood Good Shepherd's need for some cash flow, but the idea that people should be harangued about it from the pulpit truly bothered her. The pulpit was there to remind people of spirituality, not money.

How about starting a fundraiser toward a specific end? A time for people to enjoy each other's company and possibly make a donation? Something like Save Good Shepherd from the Cold and Dark.

Giving, she firmly believed, should be a choice and not forced under threat of hell.

After the meeting, she drove to the hospital to check in on Mabel Blix. The poor woman was still in her induced coma and that seriously worried Molly. She genuinely couldn't imagine the mind of anyone who would attack a woman in Mabel's condition. Or attack anyone at all, come to that.

Molly stayed for quite a while, sitting at Mabel's bedside, hoping for the slightest sign of consciousness before she decided she'd have to wait until tomorrow. She smiled and exchanged a few words with nurses and technicians as she left. The nicest thing about her job was that she had come to know quite a few people.

But as she was on her way back to the parsonage, her heart jammed into her throat.

Another house was surrounded by crime-scene tape. More lights swirled atop police cars. Tyra Lansing, one of Molly's closest friends, lived there.

And Callum's rangy figure, so unmistakable, was right in the middle of everything.

For several minutes, Molly sat with her hands gripping the steering wheel so tightly that they ached. Instead of murmuring the usual prayers, she had a stern one-sided conversation with God.

You may have set us loose with free will, but for Pete's sake, offer a hand from time to time. You protect the lilies of the field, but what about us two-legged organisms? Sure, we make our own misery, but You could still help out. That business about mankind being responsible for the world's suffering is beginning to wear thin with me.

She could have said a whole lot more, but even as she spouted her distress, she knew she was going over the top. God couldn't be blamed for violence generated by humans. Or by nature, for that matter.

Still, a visit from St. Michael with his flaming sword might do a bit of good.

She eased her car over until she was parked out of the way, then climbed out, into the waning winter afternoon, and walked to the tape, fearing what she'd hear.

Guy Redwing was standing there and greeted her with an angry face.

"Is it Tyra?" she asked, although in her heart of hearts she knew it was.

Guy nodded. "She's on her way to the hospital. I can't tell you more, Pastor."

"I know." Molly's heart squeezed until she felt as if it was being gripped by a giant fist. "What's going on?" A question without answer.

"If we knew that, we'd already have the perp. But that's obvious, isn't it." Guy's jaw tightened. "In all my years here, I've never seen the like of this. Now we have a vandal throwing rocks through store windows."

Molly gasped. "Really?"

"Drive down Main Street. Freitag's Mercantile lost three windows last night. Melinda's bakery window is cracked. Lucky, I guess, that she has a double-paned window."

What in the world was happening?

And it all seemed worse, somehow, given the time of year. Which was a ridiculous thought.

"Got any good ideas for Christmas?" Guy asked. "Right now I'm not feeling a whole lot of holiday spirit."

"Me, either." Thoughts of decorating her tree had fallen away.

Then she squared her shoulders. She had other people to think about, people who might now grow scared. People who deserved to feel some of the joy of this season.

"Listen, Guy," she said after a moment, "I know Tyra wouldn't want anyone to lose their pleasure in the holiday. Especially the kids. They shouldn't have to deal with this."

Guy nodded slowly. "You're right, Pastor. Let's think of the kids."

It helped. Some. But Molly felt nearly crushed, anyway.

Tyra. Oh, God, Tyra, too? She still felt stunned and slammed the door after she reached the parsonage and stepped inside.

It was not a good time to be alone, but anger still trickled through her, and she had no desire to seek comfort in the church.

She looked upward again. "St. Michael. Just for a few minutes."

Then she eyed her tree and decided to get to it. This weekend, children would be coming by the church to enjoy hot drinks and to practice singing Christmas carols. Every year, the youngsters walked around town and sang on street corners. An old tradition that hadn't died here. A tradition she loved as much as she loved the others.

But some of those children would want to see her tree. She also needed to bake gingerbread men for them.

Mentally, she rolled up her sleeves, put on one of her CDs of carols and set to work.

Chapter Four

Night had deepened by the time Callum left the crime scene. One of the deputies had reported that Tyra Lansing was still unconscious. Head trauma. Broken ribs. A broken arm.

Whoever had done this was enjoying the pain he inflicted. Savoring it. Seeing it as the end in itself.

Because once again nothing of value had been taken as far as anyone could tell.

Neighbors had seen nothing. Well, why would they in the dark hours of winter? Every normal person was indoors, likely snuggled in bed. With windows closed, they wouldn't hear anything, either.

And all the police had were some heavy boot prints in the snow of the alley. All that told them was that the guy was big. Given how snow compressed, it was hard to guess how heavy he might be.

So okay, they likely had a male perp. Surprise, surprise.

Callum could have waited until morning, but he didn't want to. Simple as that.

He was chilled to the bone despite the high-quality winter gear he'd purchased for this climate. A sticky web of self-loathing tightened around him, even though he knew his guilt was unreasonable.

And he didn't want to spend another night with a glass of bourbon and a hideous spread of photos on his coffee table.

He had a reason for his visit, though. A number of neighbors had said that Tyra Lansing was good friends with Molly Canton. He definitely needed to talk to her and persuaded himself that she was probably a great deal less busy at this time of evening. Even though he had no idea how busy she was.

Half of him hoped she wouldn't answer her door when he knocked. That she was in the church building busy with something. Half of him knew damn well he shouldn't be here.

But the door opened and he faced a Molly Canton dusted with flour, a bit even smeared on her cheeks, and surrounded by a mouth-watering aroma.

She started to smile that warm smile but it died half-born, seemingly replaced by tension. "It's about Tyra. How bad?"

"I just have a few questions, that's all. No news about Ms. Lansing."

She nodded, relief flooding her face. "Well, come in out of the cold. I just pulled a batch of gingerbread men from the oven and I'm sure a few would taste good with coffee or tea."

Given the aroma, he figured they'd taste good with nothing at all. "Thanks," he said as he followed her into her tiny kitchen and unzipped his parka. "It sure does smell good in here."

"Well, hike up a chair and sit," she told him, her smile returning. She turned and used a spatula to move a few cookies from a cooling rack and onto a small floral plate. As she passed it to him, she asked, "Coffee or tea?"

"Don't go to any trouble for me."

She tsked. "Which is your poison? At this point I'd like either one myself. I have too many cookies left to bake, cool and put away to get sleepy now."

"Coffee, please. And why are you baking so many?"

She glanced over her shoulder as she started the coffee maker. "Children."

"Children?" Was she hiding them somewhere?

"On Saturday, the kids have a choir rehearsal to prepare for when they go caroling around town. Part of this is a tradition...well, I guess it's *my* tradition because I haven't been here that long and this is only my second Christmas. Anyway, after the rehearsal some of the kids come over to see my tree, and part of it is plucking gingerbread men off the tree to eat."

"Sounds like a good tradition."

"The rest of the cookies will go on the tree in the church hall in the basement. We'll see if I'm here long enough to make it traditional."

He had just been about to bite into one of the cookies but stopped. "Why wouldn't you be here long enough?"

"Let's just leave it that a woman pastor isn't exactly ideal for this county. In fairness, though, it's getting better." Smiling, she brought him coffee, then sat across from him.

Well, that stank, he thought. Must have been miserable to start here with a bunch of people resenting her.

"These are great," he told her sincerely after eating a cookie. Memories nearly swamped him. At this point he couldn't tell if they were uplifting or depressing, but Angela had always baked her way through the holidays. She'd absolutely loved to bake. God, he missed her.

"But about Tyra," Molly said, rising as a timer dinged. She bent to pull another sheet of cookies from the oven. "How is she? Really."

"Really? Really she's a mess and still unconscious, like Ms. Blix. This perp is loaded with anger, would be my guess, a cocked pistol. Or maybe he's just a serious sadist. Speculation on my part."

"You probably have the experience to speculate." Her expression grew so sad. "But you said you had some questions for me."

He nodded, reached for a paper napkin from a stack at the end of the table. "People are saying you're good friends with Ms. Lansing."

"I am. Drawn close, I think, because we're both outsiders." She slipped more cookies onto the cooling rack and another sheet into the oven. Tall stacks of cooled gingerbread men filled two large plates.

He arched an eyebrow. "Outsiders?"

"Well, you know about me," she answered, then her tone grew dry. "And, of course, Tyra is Black, which is not common in Conard County."

"Why should her race make a difference?" He knew it was a ridiculous question, but he wanted to hear her take.

Molly simply shook her head. "I'm sure it's different in Boston, but around here most people are Caucasian. We have a smattering of Indigenous people, of course, but Tyra is pretty much a singularity around here." Then she eyed him. "I doubt you're uneducated about race relations."

"I'm not. Plenty of tension that doesn't need to exist."

"We are in agreement about that."

"So how did Ms. Lansing get here and why doesn't she leave?"

"She came for a teaching job at the high school. She loves it. Anyway, there haven't been any problems and she's highly respected. Her students seem to love her as much as she loves her teaching. She's a great person."

He decided to reach for another cookie. "Any reason anyone would want to hurt her the way they hurt Ms. Blix? Enemies? Exes? Disputes?"

Molly's brow wrinkled. "Not that I'm aware of. Which doesn't mean anything, I guess. I'm sure I have enemies of my own but they haven't done anything to let me know."

Callum sat back, mug in hand, resisting the urge to eat that last cookie on the plate she'd given him. It must have been hard for her to be a pioneer, as the first woman pastor around here. Lonely. Frustrating. She had to be a stubborn and patient woman.

Molly spoke again. "So why did you come here from Boston?"

One corner of his mouth lifted reluctantly. "Less mayhem."

That drew a quiet laugh from her. "I guess I should wish you luck."

"So it seems."

The atmosphere was starting to get cozy, and Callum knew he should leave before the mood resurrected more memories. Like of the old house he and Angela had been slowly restoring to an earlier glory. Like the evenings in the kitchen, while Angela baked delights that she often gave away. He got the cleaning-up part. Other evenings in the living room with a glass of wine, music playing, easy, lazy conversation flowing.

Yeah, he'd better leave now. But just as he started to rise, Molly spoke.

"You know," she said slowly, "if Tyra had been the first victim instead of Mabel, I'd be harboring awful suspicions."

"Understandable." He relaxed into the chair again and waited to see if there was more information. Focusing on his job got him through a lot of sad moments.

"Even so," she remarked briskly, "the suspicions are bad enough." Then she stood, clearly ending the evening.

He rose, too, and extended his hand for a shake. "Thanks for the cookies. And if you think of anything at all, let me know." He left his newly minted card on her table and headed for the front door.

As he stepped out and turned to close it behind himself, he saw Molly standing there.

She smiled. "I don't mean to be so abrupt, but in my position I have to be careful about perceptions."

"I should have thought of that before I came over." He should have, although coming from a very different world, it hadn't occurred to him.

"Not that I wouldn't stand up to them—" she shrugged "—but why look for a fight?"

She probably had enough of them already, he thought as he walked away into swirling snow. More than enough.

FOR NEARLY THE first time since moving here, when Molly closed the door behind Callum she felt as if the house was big and empty. It was an odd sensation for such a small cottage.

Still, she felt it. The lights on the tree in the living room twinkled invitingly, and after she'd put the remaining dough in the refrigerator and covered the baked cookies with plastic wrap, she took full advantage of that tree.

Her predecessor had left it behind when he'd moved on to shepherd a large congregation in Omaha. With three kids, he probably needed the pay boost, she thought, grinning. Although he'd probably needed more living room, too. How he'd squeezed those three kids into this house she couldn't imagine. They'd had a dog as well.

Crowded. And probably a place they'd filled with love and laughter. Maybe. She'd heard that Reverend Stanton had belonged to the fire-breathing ranks. Maybe *that* was why the wardens had chosen a woman to fill the vacancy. A complete change of pace.

Some people, she'd discovered, vastly preferred a strict religion that promised endless punishment for failures. Others felt drawn to something much kinder and full of forgiveness. Both sides had their points, but catering to both schools could sometimes be a tightrope walk.

She sighed, wishing she could feel the least bit sleepy. Another insomnia night? Well, her homily would certainly get done well before time. Maybe she could even rustle up some fundraising ideas to settle the worried wardens.

Worried Wardens. She liked that and decided that was how she would think of them from now on. It took some of the sting out of the force they'd become in her life.

All of them meant well, she was sure, but more than one struck her as being on a bit of a power trip. Callisto Manx was the exception, but then Callisto was the exception to quite a lot. When Molly thought about it, she was still astonished that Callisto had even been elected a warden.

Maybe tides were changing even here. About time, when she considered that women were the heart and soul of every church she'd ever known.

ARTHUR KILLIAN HAD a pretty good thing going for a man who thirsted for vengeance and hadn't been able to think about much else for a long time now.

That bitch was gonna pay.

Especially since he couldn't locate the conniving, stupid, useless broad who'd been his wife. Man, he'd wasted a lot of time looking for her.

But finding Molly Canton, the only other possible object of his ire, had turned out to be comparatively easy. Oh, the National Guard hadn't been any help. Canton had been on duty when she tangled with him, but beyond the court papers, they were silent as clams.

The real eye-opener had been his web search. Only a handful of people in the entire country shared the name *Molly Canton*. Sifting through them had been easy enough—it had only taken a week to narrow his search down to those who fit the right age bracket with a military background. It cost him a few bucks to get that detailed information, but it had been worth it.

Sergeant Molly Canton, with a quick fist and well-aimed knee, had turned into a preacher. Soldier to saint. He invariably snickered when he thought about it. He bet she was soft now.

Anyway, he'd been able to settle into this small town without a problem. He'd rented a big box truck and parked it in the truck-stop lot, then had spent some time in the diner muttering about how he was stuck between the heavy snowfall and the delay in picking up his next load in Cheyenne. It easily explained his lingering, and he'd been able to find decent enough lodging at the La-Z-Rest motel. It had burned to the ground a few months ago and still stank of ash and fire, but a part of it had been rebuilt enough that he'd grabbed himself a discounted room.

Pretty well set, indeed, for the plans that he had to take care not to carry out too quickly.

But he'd taken out two women who were close to the bitch. At some point Molly Canton would realize he was after *her*. Or not. Once he got to her, it wouldn't matter.

But he thought breaking those windows had been a smart touch. Confusing the whole crime situation. Giving him plenty of ways to cover his tracks.

Chapter Five

The snowstorm overnight had delivered only six inches of snow. When Molly stepped out from the parsonage, she took a little time to admire the way the fresh white blanket gleamed and sparkled, acting like a prism so that many snowflakes reflected different colors.

Jimmy Dawson had apparently arrived bright and early, since the walkway from the parsonage to the rear entrance of the church was already cleared and sanded. A wonderful man, Jimmy.

Inside the relative warmth of the church, she found the church secretary already at her desk, busy with papers and the daily diary.

Henrietta Gilchrist was a woman in her late fifties with a head of short white hair and a face that seemed nearly ageless. She was decked out in an oversize dark green sweater and wool pants.

"Good morning, Pastor," she said brightly. Always formal was Henrietta.

"Good morning, Henrietta. How's the day look?"

The church office itself was spacious, full of dark

antique furnishings except for the computer on Henrietta's desk. Molly much preferred her own little study at the parsonage.

"Not too full," the secretary answered. "Folks are busy getting ready for Christmas. Tomorrow will be different, however. One wedding and two christenings."

Those were celebrations Molly would need to attend. "But I don't need to push anything aside? I'd like to go visit Mabel Blix and Tyra Lansing."

"Plenty of room today. I can clear more for tomorrow if you want. Some of these home visits can wait. But don't forget the choir rehearsal tonight."

"I can't miss that."

Henrietta shook her head. "Absolutely not. Oh, and the new market is offering precooked hams for the Christmas supper and quite a few boxes of stuffing and dried mashed potatoes. The volunteer list is on the rise."

That lifted Molly's heart. Being able to provide a special meal to those who couldn't provide their own was a good thing. The kind of thing they needed to do more often, but a regular soup kitchen was beyond them. It was hard enough to get dried goods to pass out the rest of the year.

"That's good news," she told Henrietta.

"I'll keep working on it. Some folks just need to be reminded. Now you take yourself over to the hospital. I'm so worried about those two women. I can't imagine why this happened."

Molly couldn't, either, but imagining why didn't change the facts one bit.

The hospital brought her more good news. Both women were awake. On pain meds, but still conscious. Molly headed for Mabel's room first, where she found Callum McCloud with his notebook out.

"I really don't know what happened," Mabel told him, her voice slightly slurred from the medication. "I'm not sure how much is that I can't remember. I just know I was sleeping. I always keep the lights on because it's safer for me to get around at night, so you would think I saw something, but all I remember was a blow to my head. I didn't see who did it. It came from behind while I was lying down. After that I don't recall a thing until I woke up."

Callum nodded and slipped his notebook into his jacket pocket. "If you remember anything more, will you be sure to have someone call me? We want to find this guy."

"Thank you," Mabel murmured, growing sleepier. "Pastor Molly…" Her voice trailed off completely.

"You can try coming back in an hour or so," the nurse told them. "She'll be in and out most of the day."

Outside the room, Molly looked at Callum. "Have you talked to Tyra?"

"I was just about to."

"Is it all right if I come?"

He offered her that half smile that didn't reach his eyes. "As if I could keep you out."

"Well, at least we have an understanding about that."

"They're part of your flock. You can do more for them than I can."

"At least for now."

Tyra was only three rooms down and was sitting up with a bed tray in front of her, her breakfast only half-touched. She smiled when she saw Molly. "Wondered when you'd get here, girl."

"I was here yesterday, but you ignored me."

Tyra gave a short, pained laugh. "I was ignoring everything." She looked at Callum.

"Detective Callum McCloud," he said, introducing himself.

"Oh, you're the new guy everyone wonders about. You'd better tell them a little more about yourself or they'll be making up their own stories."

Molly sat in the chair beside the bed and took Tyra's hand gently. "How are you feeling?"

"Like a mule kicked me more than once. But I'll be fine. I just hate being away from the school right now. Those kids will be bouncing with excitement." She looked at Callum. "Even the older ones get wound up for Christmas. Some get irritated by it, but I just enjoy it. You'd be surprised how many of them don't get very happy the rest of the year."

"I wouldn't be surprised at all."

Tyra nodded, her long, intricate braids dancing on the pillow. "I bet you have questions for me."

"Anything at all that you can remember."

Tyra frowned and let her head fall back against the pillow. "Guy seemed to come out of nowhere."

"Guy?"

"Yeah. Kinda bulky, but who can be sure under those parkas. Just an impression. I couldn't sleep and was making a cup of tea. I saw something move in a reflection from the kitchen window, I turned around and then *boom*! Side of my head felt like it was imploding."

Callum spoke sympathetically. "It was a pretty bad blow."

"Tell me about it," Tyra said dryly.

"Was the man wearing anything that stood out to you?"

"No. All black with a balaclava under his parka hood."

"Eye color?"

Tyra closed her eyes. "Blueish, maybe. It was only a quick glimpse. They were certainly lighter than dark brown."

"Height?"

"A little taller than me. I'm five-nine."

"Can you think of anyone who might want to hurt you?"

Tyra gave it a minute's thought. "Not that I'm aware of, although I did get into quite an argument with a father who didn't think I should be passing out copies of *To Kill a Mockingbird* as an English assignment. I doubt anyone would want to do this to me over a book, though."

"His name?"

"Reedy. Gerry Reedy."

Callum put away his notebook, looking satisfied. "You've been a great help, Ms. Lansing. If you remember anything else, just call me." He placed a card on her table. "Or ask anyone at all to call me for you. I'll leave you with the pastor now."

Molly squeezed Tyra's hand as Callum walked out. "I wish I could give you a hug."

Tyra managed an impish smile. "Please don't. I'll take it as a given."

Molly felt the ache rising in her heart again, replacing the joy she'd first felt at learning both women were recovering. "I'm so sorry this happened to you."

"Me, too," Tyra answered frankly. "I just hope it doesn't happen to anyone else. How's Mabel doing?"

"Still in and out on the medications but improving."

"That's good news." Tyra sighed. "I'm getting sleepy again, but that's okay now. You get back to your duties and let me heal, girl. I'll be knocking on your door again before you know it."

"You better be."

"And Molly? Don't let this ruin your holiday for you. I know how much you love it. What you might do is drip some of that joy into that detective. Looks like he needs it."

That was Tyra, bless her. Always thinking of others.

Outside in the cold, she was surprised to see Callum, as if he was waiting for her.

"You need me?" she asked.

"Tyra's information was helpful," he remarked. "The eyes and height of the assailant. Interesting, though, that both women were attacked in the light. You'd expect someone like this to be working in the dark."

"That would make sense. Apparently none of this makes sense."

"No." He sighed. "Anyway, you know a whole lot of people. Do me a favor and pay attention to anything you hear or see. Someone might have some wisp of knowledge that could prove useful."

"I hope so."

The beautiful blue sky of the early morning had given way to pregnant clouds. A light snowfall swirled gently. Callum walked away, appearing lost in deep thought, and Molly headed back to the church. She was sure that Henrietta had been being kind when she said today's schedule was light. It wasn't often the case.

When she arrived back at Good Shepherd, she found Henrietta sitting with Callisto Manx in the church office. A couple of women occupied the pews, clearly deeply in prayer, so she left them alone while she closed the door and greeted Callisto.

Molly had always thought Callisto to be a striking woman—tall, strongly boned and wearing a black bob that appeared to be from another era. It suited the shape of Callisto's face perfectly.

"To what do I owe the honor?" Molly asked Callisto as she sat at her own desk.

"Friendship," Callisto said wryly. "I thought you should know that the ladies' Altar Society is in the middle of a tussle that's not getting any prettier. It's bound to spill on you, so take this as a heads-up so you can prepare yourself."

Molly nodded. The was not the first time she'd faced a set-to like this and it was bound not to be the last. "What's going on?"

"Janice Remy is titular head of the group, as you know. But Claire AuCoin is the de facto head. And by that, I mean everyone listens to Claire and follows her directions. I'm sure you've noticed. In any event, the problem blew up when Claire asked Georgia to darn the edges of the Christmas altar cloth and Janice announced that Claire had no right to do any such thing."

Molly nodded her head. "The group should be cooperative, shouldn't they?"

"You'd think. But it's the same trying to get the Senior Warden and Junior Warden to agree on anything except that you're wrong somehow. I personally believe that the church is no place for power struggles."

"But people will be people," Molly acknowledged.

"Sadly. I just wanted you to be ready for it when it really blows up. Then, I gave Daniel Alder a piece of my mind. For heaven's sake, as Junior Warden, finances are his headache. Why should he dump all that on you? So I told him to straighten up and do his job."

Molly drew a sharp breath, trying not to laugh. "You didn't."

"I did. And John Jason is next on my list. He's the Senior Warden but all he does is try to stir up trouble in one way or another."

Molly shook her head. "Be careful, Callisto. They could throw you off the Vestry."

"See if I care. They won't be able to shut my mouth and I swear if they pull that I'll be talking outside vestry meetings."

With a *harrumph*, Callisto rose. Then she smiled at Molly. "You're doing a very good job, Pastor. Many of us have your back."

After the door closed, Henrietta made a sound of disapproval. Molly eyed her.

"What's wrong, Henrietta?"

"Bringing politics through this door is all."

"Politics are part of human nature."

"Be that as it may—" Henrietta frowned "—they don't belong in here."

"Seeing as how they are part of human nature, they *will* come in here, and my job is not to ignore it, but to try to keep this congregation together."

"Good luck dealing with this lot. The Vestry is bad enough but to have the Altar Society at each other's throats could spread all over the place."

Into factions. But Molly didn't say that. Like any other organization, there were groups of friends, tightly knit. If they started taking sides, life could get fractious indeed.

"No Christmas spirit," Henrietta muttered. "Ugly things have happened, and I know they burden your heart, but don't let them steal the joy from you. Don't let *anyone* do that."

"How's your Christmas spirit doing?" Molly asked.

Henrietta smiled brightly. "The family is coming! They weren't sure they could but I'll get to see my grandchildren."

"That's the best happiness of all."

CHOIR REHEARSAL THAT evening was beautiful. Good Shepherd had a wonderful choir, but the carols brought out something more in them. And at the candlelight service on Christmas Eve, with the entire congregation joining in, the experience would become indescribably moving.

She spoke to the choir afterward, telling them how beautiful they sounded and thanking them for the effort. She gave a short, impromptu homily about this time of love and peace, then shook hands at the door as everyone departed.

Only a few expressed concern about the victimization of two women, but she did her best to reassure them. As if anything short of arresting the creep could do that.

After a time spent in solitary prayer asking for blessings while kneeling before the altar, she headed back to the parsonage and stopped short when she saw Callum McCloud.

"Did something happen?" she asked immediately, her heart skipping a beat.

"Nothing worrisome." He tilted his head. "Like a kid, I came hoping for more cookies and coffee."

She laughed and opened the door to him. "I think that can be arranged."

But now she realized that Callum was truly a lonely man. A sad one.

She had to find a way to help him beyond cookies and coffee.

CALLUM FELT LIKE a bit of a fool, dropping in like this, but it was as if he'd been inexorably drawn. His bachelor pad had little to offer even when he didn't face bleak crimes, and something in him was reaching out.

He didn't know if that was a good thing, but Molly's door seemed like a safe one to knock on.

This time she offered him coffee and cookies in her tiny living room, where they could see her Christmas tree. He settled on a recliner that had seen better days. It certainly needed at least one spring repaired. But nothing in this house appeared to be in much better condition.

When she had served and settled, she waxed about the choir rehearsal and how wonderful it had been. Then she made the inevitable invitation to the candlelight service.

He'd known he was going to be invited to her church sooner or later. The problem was that since his wife's death he had absolutely no desire to go into a church. Or anywhere near one.

When there was no hope in the world, faith seemed like a false promise. A delusion.

"I'll think about it," he answered her, offering no commitment but not refusing outright. There was no point in telling her what he really thought.

"Tomorrow's going to be busy," she remarked. "Two baptisms and a wedding. I'll have to be careful not to overindulge the bubbly at the celebrations afterward."

"One toast?" he asked.

"That's safe enough." Her smile was bright. "New beginnings. I love them!"

He nodded, wishing he could find the smile she deserved, but failing. He certainly didn't want to tell her this was the worst time of year for him. From everything he'd seen so far, he guessed this might be her favorite time.

"It's so beautiful," she continued, "the fresh snow-fall last night. So clean and pristine, and I love the way the air smells. The way sounds are muffled. A hush seems to settle over the whole world."

"It does," he agreed. Then, before the gushing continued—mostly for his benefit, he thought—he said, "How's your congregation taking the two attacks?"

"We haven't had Sunday service yet, so I haven't seen most of them. But tonight after choir practice, only a few expressed fears. For most, that's human nature, thinking it can never happen to you."

"That may be true for women who don't live alone." He watched her face darken a bit. "I'm sorry, but you need to take extra care, Molly."

After a moment, she shook her head. "I'm not going to let this beast control me. As a pastor, I have important duties and my flock deserves a pastor who performs them, not one cowering in fear."

"I'm not suggesting cowering. I'm suggesting extra caution."

"Like what? Keeping my lights turned off?"

He stared at her. "I didn't say that."

"No, but you said earlier it was odd that both women had been attacked in lighted rooms. I'll grant that it's odd, but it doesn't seem like much protection to live in the dark. This guy could change his habit at any time."

He could hardly argue with that. Two similar crimes didn't even mean they'd been committed by the same perp. One could be a copycat. Or there could be one or more guys involved. Hell, even with a serial killer you couldn't even be sure you had one when there were only two crimes.

He ruminated quietly while sipping coffee and eating a second cookie. "Any link between these two victims?"

"They attend Good Shepherd. I don't even think they socialize except at church gatherings. Separate lives."

"And I bet Good Shepherd has hundreds of attendees, so that's meaningless."

Molly nodded. "All I can think of is that they're both women living alone."

"Easy targets in that sense." Time to shift gears, he decided. No reason to rain on her parade, such as it was. "Do you bake anything besides gingerbread cookies?"

"All I can say is that it's a good thing I have plenty of people to share my baking with. I may like making the stuff, but I can't eat much of it."

That weight thing again. He could have shaken his head.

"Anyway, I bake pies for the Christmas dinner, and I love to donate them wherever I can. There's a lot of satisfaction in that. It's nice to visit one of my flock with a pie. I'll bake you one soon."

"Don't go to any trouble."

"I just said I enjoy it," she replied a trifle tartly.

Again, that unusual urge to smile came over him, but he allowed only a small bit to show. "So tell me about Molly Canton. You must have done something before coming here."

"Well, I did, like most people." She rose, disappeared into her kitchen and returned with fresh coffee. "I grew up in an agnostic home," she said as she resumed her seat, a Boston rocker with a cushion. "Somehow, despite that, I found religion. Or it found me." She shrugged with a small smile.

"Then?"

"Off to college to major in social work. I joined the National Guard, too."

Callum arched an eyebrow. "Why?"

"Because I wanted to help during natural disasters."

He understood that. A lot of people felt the same— much good it did them during the war. "So how did you get here?"

"My religion became a calling. Seminary came next, followed by a church run by a pastor who *really* didn't like women of the cloth."

She flashed a grin. "Trial by fire. I survived him. Then a brief time at a smaller church with a more pleasant atmosphere. Then here. I'm still not sure why I was hired, but I'm never going to dive into that rat's nest. There are some things better left alone."

Callum nodded. "That can be very wise."

"But what about you?" she asked. "This is an odd place to come from Boston."

"Was I fired, you mean? No. I retired. Mostly I wanted to get away from those duties. Too much violence in a city." And one huge, bad memory, although his memory was already burdened with other violent crimes.

Molly sighed. "We aren't giving you a much better picture of us at the moment."

"Listen, I've been here barely three months and these are my first major crimes. No complaints."

Except he had many complaints, one of the foremost being that he didn't know the people and the area. He was working on it, but he still felt as if he had one hand tied behind his back. People knowledge had always been a great resource for him.

"It has to be hard for you to be an outsider, though," she remarked. "This area is tightly knit with relationships that go back for generations. Hard to break into, as I can attest. People are friendly enough, but I can't imagine how long you have to be here before you become a true part of the community."

"I think you're well on your way, Molly. Pastor, and all that. People must find you easier to talk with."

"I wish I could be sure." She shrugged one shoulder. "It doesn't matter. I like it here. Maybe I can finish out my career here."

Despite himself, a quiet chuckle escaped him. "Do you feel lucky?"

"Ha. We'll see. You can't please everyone."

He leaned back in the questionable chair and allowed himself to enjoy the twinkling Christmas tree. He remembered store windows in Boston filled with snowy scenes and toys to entice kids. Once, he'd found strolling those streets to be special. Then he'd become blind to them.

He knew he needed to make some mental and emotional adjustments to the greatest loss of his life, to the fact that he was still living and breathing. It was difficult, and sometimes he just wanted to wallow.

"I've kept you long enough," he said suddenly, rising to carry his plate and cup to the kitchen. "Frankly, that chair needs some respringing."

She grinned. "Jimmy's going to get to it when he has time."

"Jimmy?"

"A wonderful jack-of-all-trades. He has a family and a full-time job to look after, though. The amazing thing is that he manages to keep my walkway shoveled, as well as the entrance to the church and the parking lot."

"Good man." But from his experience, not enough.

"I think so. There are a few in the world," she joked. "Anyway, if you don't want to come to the candlelight service, come for a choir practice. It's beautiful."

"I'll see." No promise.

As he headed back through the cold clear night, knowing what awaited him on his coffee table, he wondered why he didn't just carry the load of work back to the office.

A few deputies would be there. Unfortunately, from what he'd overheard, they were planning to decorate the office.

He'd probably get dragged in.

AFTER HE GATHERED UP all his materials, he drove to the station, anyway, and hauled everything inside. As he'd feared, the deputies who were night-staffing the squad room were cheerfully hanging up window stickers and spraying snowflake stencils to leave giant flakes behind. A stuffed Santa sat in one corner and a Christmas tree in another. He even saw pieces of a reindeer waiting to be assembled. No escaping it.

"Come on," Guy Redwing said to him. "Put that briefcase on your desk and come help. You can reach the higher spaces."

"I'm not a ladder," he said, not for the first time.

"Taller than any of us. We wouldn't need to break out the ladder. And there's some hot cider and cinnamon to share."

Two of the other deputies, Randy Webster and Stu Canaday, gave him looks suggesting he'd better join them.

Well, why not? he asked himself. It was one way to get to know more people around here. And it would keep him away from those horrific photos a while longer.

"Weird about those windows being broken," Stu remarked. "That hasn't happened before."

"I know," Randy said. "I grew up around here and I've never heard of it except graduation time, when some kids get too drunk for their own good."

"Too drunk for their age," Guy said. "How many bottles do we confiscate on average?"

"Does anyone count?"

Two laughs answered him.

Callum, instead of standing on a ladder, found himself on a window ledge pasting up stickers of Santa's sleigh and reindeer. "Hey," he said. "What about the bigger Santa and deer?"

"For the other window," Guy explained. "Every window is different."

Well, that made sense. The storefront-style office of the sheriff's department offered a panoramic view of the street in front through two windows on either side of the entry door, and another facing the Courthouse Square. Plenty of room for decoration.

The hot cider was pretty good, too, and finally even Callum, who tried to keep a distance from most people, fell into the camaraderie of the activity.

"Cleaning this up is going to be a mess," Randy remarked. "It always is. We can leave the cleanup to the day shift."

Guy snorted. "How can you be sure you won't be on the day shift by morning?"

"Can't," Randy remarked equably. "Just my hope."

After spreading puffy cotton snow around the feet of the big sleigh and reindeer, everyone stood back to look at their handiwork.

"Not bad," Stu pronounced. "Not perfect, but not bad."

"Perfection is overrated," Randy joked. "Come on, let's get more cider."

Yet another thermos was opened at the coffee table. Just then, a window shattered and a brick hit the floor hard.

"Well, hell," said one of the deputies as all four of the men took off after the miscreant.

In a hurry, they left their jackets behind as they raced up the street, peering into the dark spaces of doorways and an alley. No luck, and they finally grew too cold to stay outdoors.

Guy sent out a BOLO, not that it would do much good without a description.

Cold air sucked the heat right out of the office. Everyone pulled on jackets and then the hunt for plywood began. They found a piece and hammered it into place.

"Who the hell could be this crass?" Stu asked.

"Or this stupid," remarked Guy. "Hitting this office?"

Callum responded, "He got away, didn't he?"

Grim silence answered him.

After downing half a mug of cider, Randy said, "Well, that was the prettiest window. Of course."

Of course.

Chapter Six

In the morning, a larger-than-usual group of older women showed up for morning prayer. There were even some elderly men among them.

Wondering what was going on, Molly donned her surplice and stole, and led the prayers for the day.

But the attendees didn't leave directly afterward, and two of them came up to her. "Pastor, have you heard?"

Molly raised her eyebrows and her heart raced with dread—she hoped there hadn't been another vicious attack. "Heard what?"

"Someone threw a brick through the sheriff's office window," Belinda Armistead said.

"Right as they finished decorating," Claire AuCoin added. "What is this town coming to?"

A good question, Molly thought. She hadn't been here long, but it was long enough to realize this was becoming an unusual confluence of events.

"We must pray," she said, not for the first time, "for the safety of everyone in town."

"One of the deputies could have been hurt," Belinda said. "We all need safety, God willing."

Which led to nearly a dozen people kneeling before the altar while Molly led them in prayer. She hoped they felt better, but *she* didn't.

This most joyous time of the year was beginning to turn into a nightmare.

The afternoon wedding and christenings elevated her spirits considerably. A glass of champagne at each celebration afterward made her feel a little light-headed.

New beginnings. They were always welcome. And this was certainly the time of year for them.

Two days later, Tyra was released from the hospital. Molly wanted her to stay with her in her one tiny bedroom, but Tyra would have none of it.

"It's time to get back on my feet," she announced. "I refuse to get knocked down for long. I heard Mabel isn't doing as well."

Molly shook her head sadly. "She had to go to inpatient rehab. With all her earlier problems, I guess she's going to need more help."

"Now that really makes me mad," Tyra said. "*Very* mad. That poor woman has had more than her share of misery. We've got to catch this guy."

"Callum's on it."

Tyra waved a hand. "He doesn't know this area well enough. Folks have to help him."

"I'm sure he'll appreciate any hints we can give."

Tyra turned to look at her as Molly drove down the street. "This doesn't look like the way to my house."

"It's not. I figured you couldn't refuse an apple turnover fresh from the oven."

"Oh, girl, you *do* have my number!"

And Molly had every intention of making sure Tyra stayed with her for at least a few days. She couldn't imagine that her friend honestly wanted to be alone in her own house again. Not yet, anyway. Maybe not until they caught this beast.

Regardless, the turnovers were waiting, ready to be popped into the oven. Tyra winced as she sat at the table.

"Would you prefer to sit in the living room?"

Tyra shook her head. "On those torture devices you call chairs? I think not." Then she grinned. "Truth is, these cracked ribs hurt. You put me in one of those chairs and I'm not sure I'll be able to get up. No, this is more comfortable and it's less painful to breathe."

"Cool. And you want to go home? Are you actually going to try to sleep in bed? Or sleep sitting in any of those chairs you have?"

Tyra pursed her lips. "Do I sense pressure?"

"You might."

The turnovers were soon done, covered with a sprinkling of sugar. Molly put a hot one in front of Tyra. "Don't burn your mouth."

"As if."

Just then, someone knocked on the door. Molly promptly went to answer it and was surprised to see Callum.

"Come in and join us for turnovers," she invited. "I was about to make coffee, too."

"I'm a coffee fiend," Tyra said from the kitchen. "What brings you this way, Detective?"

He hung his jacket on a peg near the door, revealing a dark blue sweater and jeans, and entered the tiny kitchen. "I came to see how you're doing."

"And if I remember any more than I told you," Tyra retorted.

Callum tipped his head. "And that, too, although I was checking on Molly and didn't know you were here. I heard about Ms. Blix. Rehab?"

"Again." Molly frowned. "She's already been through it since her car accident. In fact, she was still getting in-home therapy. Now this. I'll be visiting her, for what little comfort I can offer at this point."

"She seems to have a big blank about the entire event."

Molly placed a turnover in front of him while the coffeepot gurgled behind her.

Tyra said, "Lucky her, actually. Who needs to remember any bit of it? Might be useful to you, Detective, but not to her."

"Callum, please. And you're right. But I have a job to do, and any scrap of information can help. Right now I don't have anything to work with except your description."

"Which could be anyone at all." Tyra sighed, but not deeply. "Well, there's one more little thing that probably won't help, either. The guy smelled like Bigfoot."

That brought a laugh from Molly and the faintest of smiles from Callum.

"You know Bigfoot?" he asked.

"Not personally, but I've heard about his smell.

This guy smelled rank, like he hadn't showered in months. Of course, that could have been his clothes."

Callum nodded and pulled out his notebook from his shirt pocket, then made a note. "Smelling like that could make him very noticeable."

"Debatable around here," Tyra said dryly. "Some of these hired hands come to town and you wonder if they've ever heard of soap and water."

Conversation moved on to more pleasant matters, with Tyra complaining that she wasn't allowed to go back to work for a week. "I miss my kids, especially right now. You wouldn't believe a group of teens could get so excited about Christmas. I kind of expected them to be blasé about the entire subject. Nope."

"It shows up in church, too," Molly said. "We always have so many volunteers for the youth choir. I wish they'd hang around for the rest of the year."

"These apple turnovers are the best," Callum remarked. "You trying to put Melinda's bakery out of business?"

"Not likely. These were specially made for Tyra." Then she had a thought. "Do you cook?"

"For myself, you mean? Not likely." He rose, thanking her for the coffee and turnover, then disappeared out the door like the shadow he seemed to try to remain.

"Something about that man," Tyra remarked.

"A heavy burden," Molly mused. "Very heavy."

ARTHUR KILLIAN FELT very proud of himself. That brick through the window of the sheriff's office had been brilliant. It had undoubtedly made a lot of deputies furious because it was a clear assault on their authority. More angry than the other broken windows. He was sure that more of them were busy hunting a vandal than the assailant of two women. Especially since he hadn't attacked anyone in a few days.

His hope was that they believed he had moved on. That angry or mischievous kids were responsible for the vandalism.

That suited his plan to perfection. *Distraction.* He'd wanted it all along to protect himself. To muddy the waters.

And this dang motel room wasn't that bad, despite the ashy smell. Hasty's diner across the road sure made some good meals.

If he didn't have another purpose, he could have stayed here until he was broke.

But some things were more important than his comfort. Far more important.

He popped open a carryout container and began to dive into a heap of fries and a couple of hamburgers. And tomorrow there'd be plenty of pancakes and syrup. A guy could definitely get used to this.

MOLLY WASN'T OVERWORKED. In one way, being at a smaller church had advantages. She had ample time to write her homilies, to spend with congregants who showed up wishing for some prayer or comfort. She also had time to visit those who were housebound.

Today was her day to go visit Stacy Withers, who was dying of cancer, and Marcia Lathrop, who needed some serious help dealing with her father, who was not only difficult, but also appeared to be sinking into some serious senility.

Finding people who were willing to make trips to these outlying ranches during the heavy winter season wasn't proving easy. Many murmured sympathy and concern, but none volunteered.

Too risky on these roads to undertake scheduled visits.

But today the roads were clear and Molly set out with some turnovers in tins beside her, some magazines and a couple of her thriller novels. Stacy seemed to like those.

In-town visits were so much easier, but these trips to outlying ranches were no less important. Maybe she even felt better about them because of the difficulties they presented.

Unfortunately, she now had time to think about Callum McCloud. He was, apart from his difficulty in smiling, an extremely attractive man. She tried not to notice such things. It wasn't as if a pastor couldn't fall in love, but being a woman made matters far more precarious for her.

She certainly couldn't have an affair. The thought brought a furtive grin to her face. Such matters hadn't always been so difficult in her life. During her time in college and in the National Guard, she'd had several serious relationships. No concern about appearances back then.

But appearances ruled her life in many ways now. She sometimes had to remind herself that she'd chosen this life and its sacrifices.

And there were sacrifices. A penurious allowance, life in a cottage that needed some serious renovations and time that wasn't often her own.

She had to be available as much as possible. She had to remain in the church office in case someone needed to speak with her. Yes, she had some freedom, but for the sake of her flock, she kept that freedom on a short leash.

But Callum had caught her attention more than anyone else she remembered. And once again, she decided she needed to help him out somehow.

By the time she finished her visits and was on her way home, gentle snow had begun to fall once more. More snow than last year, she thought, but she didn't have much of a comparison.

It was with warmth that she saw Good Shepherd rise before her. She felt as if she was coming home.

CALLUM'S THOUGHTS WERE running along a different line. He kept getting the feeling that the window vandalism and the attacks on the two women were related somehow.

But such different crimes from the same perp? Even two?

How unlikely could that get?

Still, after all his years in policing, he was reluctant to ignore niggles of intuition. Something was going very wrong in Conard City from what he could determine, and his fellow officers were quick to share that feeling with him.

They were perplexed, as he was, but troubled because this seemed like a veritable crime wave in their small town. Maybe it was.

Even the sheriff, Gage Dalton, was growing cranky about it. "Get to it, people," he'd said only that morning. "This can't continue."

But even the brick that had come through the department's window offered no clues except that it must have come from the abandoned train depot on the edge of town. Dusting for fingerprints didn't help, of course. Gloves. In this weather, even foolish teens would be wearing gloves.

In the sheriff's private office, Gage regarded Callum across his desk. He spoke in a gravelly voice, no smile on his burn-scarred face. "It seems we've given you quite a conundrum for your first major case with us."

"So it seems," Callum answered. "Usually, though, someone screws up and leaves a useful clue behind."

"But how long do we have to wait for that?" Gage tapped his pencil on his desk, a habit Callum had already grown used to. "Lousy time of year to have our citizens getting upset and worried. The serious worry is going to start soon if we don't get a break. If there's another assault, fear will take over. Merry Christmas."

While Callum had plenty of reason not to care about Christmas, he knew others did and he didn't want it ruined for them. Not that he honestly felt any other time of year would be better.

"Poor Pastor Molly," Gage said, surprising him.

"Why 'poor pastor'?"

Gage managed a crooked smile. "She loves the

Christmas season, and as we all saw last year, she does her best to make it magical for everyone else. This year is probably going to be harder for her."

Callum nodded, not knowing what else to say.

Gage sighed and leaned forward. "Connie's out front. You asked her to compile a list of women who live alone around here. I think she's completed it. One starting point, anyway. Maybe the only one."

CONNIE PARISH WAS USEFUL, not only in compiling the list, but she'd also offered to arrange drive-bys on a more regular basis by uniformed officers from both the city police and county sheriff's office.

Callum accepted the offer readily, but he doubted it would be helpful. This guy struck in the night, and apparently only in houses with lights on. The strangest modus operandi he'd ever seen or heard of.

"Connie, let's keep those patrols thickest at night around houses with lights on, okay?"

She nodded. "Makes sense. Will do."

"And I suggest these officers make a point of stopping at all the houses of the single women to encourage them to keep a better eye out. Or arrange pajama parties. Whatever."

When he stepped out of the office, into another quiet snowfall, he felt no more enlightened or useful than before.

Damn, there *had* to be a link between these two crimes. Some reason these two women had been chosen. Even serial killers had motives, however twisted they might be and there was no reason this type of perp should be any different.

When he reached the corner, before getting into his unmarked car, he stopped, barely aware of the snow falling around him. A bad, sad time of year, he thought. Full of promise for others, but not for him.

Angela. She was never far from his mind, a murder scene he'd stepped into before anyone could prevent him. A hideousness that haunted his days and nights. A horror that never quite slipped from his mind.

He knew he should be moving past it. With every breath he drew, with every step he took, he was choosing to live. But that life had to involve something more than work and memories, didn't it?

And maybe he had some kind of duty to find those things somehow. He thought of Molly baking gingerbread cookies to decorate her tree for children. Of sharing an apple turnover with him and Tyra.

Of the night he had simply gone there to ask for a cookie, like some kid. A night he had needed the comfort of another soul, and Molly had a cheerful, warm, welcoming heart.

It had been, he admitted, the first time he'd reached out to anyone for any kind of comfort since Angela. Not that people hadn't tried to offer it, but he hadn't been ready to accept any.

So he'd come here to be a stranger. Not to flee Angela—he'd never flee his memories of her. They meant too much. But to get away from the constant reminders, where every little thing held too many warm remembrances? Yes. To escape a job that had become overwhelming when it struck too close to home? Yes.

Now this. The case of these women was like walking back into his worst nightmare, and at the same time of year. It would have been easy to become a Scrooge, but Molly kept yanking him back from that even if she didn't know it.

Though she clearly identified him as a troubled man, that didn't prevent her from smiling or talking about her delight in the season. He sure as hell didn't want to put a damper on that.

But his primary concern had to be the attacks on these two women. And the intuition that the broken windows were part of the larger whole.

But how and why? Nothing was adding up. Women in lighted rooms rather than dark ones. Why? Broken windows. Why?

Nothing fit, and that bothered him more than anything could.

A slightly taller man, Tyra had said. Coming from behind her while she stood at her kitchen sink. Stinking to high heaven.

Bigfoot. The name ought to stick, especially considering the size of the footprints they'd found at both scenes.

Bigfoot. And just about as elusive.

BACK IN THE church basement, Molly helped the children make angels out of paper doilies and pieces of ribbon. The figures lacked wings, but they were still identifiable by their shapes, and the kids had a great time. They all took some home with them for their own trees. Laura Maskin, the retired teacher, and her aide, Belinda Armistead, both looked happy as the kids departed and they began the inevitable cleanup. Somehow scissors and glue had gotten involved, although how Molly couldn't say, as she helped straighten everything up.

Then she went upstairs for evening prayer. Attendance was light, but there were some smiling faces who stayed after for a few minutes, and people invited her to various gatherings at their homes for a little good cheer.

It all sounded nice, but Molly couldn't think of a way to accept any of those invitations without eventually offending others that would follow if it became known she had accepted any. Instead, she suggested a gathering in the church hall in the next few days, one that wasn't scheduled, for anyone who cared to come.

"Don't forget the cider," she called after the departing families. "And let people know."

After a little straightening-up around the altar, Molly pulled on her jacket over her clerical garb and headed back to the parsonage. Time to do some more baking, especially if there was to be a gathering in a couple of days. Then there were the final touches around the church that she needed to think about.

No outdoor or indoor colored lights, of course, but more candlesticks to be wrapped with red and white bows. Maybe she could find those white wire angels that someone had donated last year. They carried big faux gold trumpets and added a nice touch outside the front doors.

Once indoors, warming up, she played "Hark! The Herald Angels Sing" because the song always cheered her up.

But why did she need cheering? Because of Mabel and Tyra, of course.

Tyra, who'd yielded to pleas to stay with Molly for a few days, stumbled out of the very tiny ground-floor bedroom, her robe wrapped tightly around her.

"What's got into you?" Tyra asked sleepily. "Trying to wake all the angels?"

Molly immediately felt guilty. "I'm sorry, I forgot you might be sleeping."

"You forgot I was here." Tyra yawned. "Which is good, I guess. Any possibility of tea?"

"Sure. Maybe you'll wake up enough to help me tie ribbons around the gingerbread men."

Tyra slid into a kitchen chair, yawning again. "As long as it's not around their necks. Not a pretty image."

"Under their arms," Molly assured her.

"But no frosting?"

"Heck no. Sticky fingers."

Tyra laughed carefully, sleepily. "Tea. Remember?"

Grateful for her electric kettle, Molly filled it with water and turned it on. "Green or black tea?"

"Green. Better for the heart, I hear."

Tyra slumped a little, resting her chin in her palm. "The good news is that I managed to get into bed without screaming from my ribs. The bad news is that I almost screamed when I got up."

Molly flushed. "I'm so sorry!"

"For what? For the fact that you're one of Santa's

elves at this time of year? Be happy, enjoy it. Life provides little enough of those opportunities." She smiled drowsily. "It was nice to wake up to, all that musical joy. Have at it."

With the tea poured, Molly was about to sit with Tyra when someone knocked at her door. Glancing at the clock, she saw it was just before ten. "I hope it's not an emergency," she said as she hurried to answer it. Her heart always skipped a few beats when someone arrived so late. A death in the family? That was always her biggest worry.

Instead, she found Guy Redwing standing there, so buttoned up against the cold that he might have been a snowman himself.

"Sorry to bother you, Pastor, but Detective McCloud wants us to warn single women not to leave their lights on."

Molly nodded. "Sounds weird, but I understand why. Would you like to join Tyra and me for a few minutes to warm up?"

Guy flashed her a smile. "If I hold still too long I'll freeze in place. You might ask McCloud, though. I saw him just down the street. He's walking so you can bet he's colder than I am."

Molly laughed. "Well, tell him the welcome mat is out."

"Always is at your place." Guy gave her a mittened salute then turned and left.

"Poor guy," Tyra remarked. "I wouldn't want to be out there doing his job right now."

"Me, either, although I'd bet from what he said that *he's* got a car."

Tyra asked for more tea and if Molly had any turnovers left. Of course, she did, and it wasn't as if she was going to eat any herself.

"How many diets have you been on?" Tyra asked as she watched Molly serve only one plate.

"As many as have been invented. I think."

Tyra chuckled. "You are out of your mind."

"My stomach and the scale disagree. Frankly, I don't want to look matronly."

Tyra shook her head. "Probably helps in your job, though." Then she bit into a turnover. "You can make me a batch of these any time the urge overcomes you."

"Yeah, but you were blessed with being tall and lean."

"And you were blessed with being short and cute."

Another knock at the door interrupted them. This time it was Callum. "Guy said the welcome mat is out."

His cheeks were red from the cold and his hair was a bit tousled. Molly bet he hadn't even been wearing a hat.

Molly ushered him in with a smile. "Quickly. Don't let the heat out." Still in her clerical blouse and slacks, she felt just a bit self-conscious. She wondered if his aversion to the church extended to pastoral clothing.

He knocked snow off his boots before stepping inside, then saw Tyra as he was pulling off his jacket. "Hey, Tyra. How are you doing?"

"I've got some slightly used ribs I can sell cheap. Other than that, I'm doing much better. And these turnovers, unless I miss my bet, are still filling Molly's plastic container. We're drinking tea, though."

"I can make coffee," Molly said quickly. "It's not like it's a tough chore."

"Tea is fine," Callum assured her. "I was just here to check up on you two, but Guy caught up with me. I suppose I could have just left you in your peace."

"I'm glad you didn't," Molly said cheerfully. "The more the merrier. But what are you doing walking around out there so late?"

"Getting cold."

Molly laughed. Tyra could barely manage a snort.

"But seriously, what's going on?" Molly asked.

"Nothing at the moment, thankfully. No, just walking because it helps me think."

Tyra spoke. "No thinking in a frozen brain."

Molly placed tea and two turnovers in front of Callum. "Dig in. So no more attacks?"

"No. Maybe they're over. We did find a partial fingerprint at Mabel Blix's house, but just one. We've sent it in for analysis but that will take a while. And if the perp isn't on AFIS, the national database, no help at all. Regardless, we'd have to match the print to someone we think did the crime."

"Not as easy as on TV."

"Little is. So you're feeling better, Tyra?"

Tyra tossed her long black braids. "Better enough to get around. Although the bed is still an instrument of torture."

Callum winced. "I can imagine."

"It just takes time to mend," Tyra answered. "Although Molly woke me up with Christmas music. I swear there's no dampening of this woman's happiness at this time of year."

Callum looked at Molly, his face revealing nothing, as usual. "That's a good thing."

Molly bridled. "Is it? On the one hand I have a congregation that deserves to enjoy Christmas, and on the other I'm sickened by these attacks. Just sickened. I hope to heaven I never meet this guy because I might forget my Christian principles. Turning the other cheek is a great teaching but one of the hardest to follow, and I'm no different."

Tyra groaned softly as she reached over to cover Molly's hand with hers. "I'm sure you'd be forgiven."

"I wish I was as sure." She paused, her mind shooting into her past. "Life has taught me a lot of things, you know. Not every one of them is kind, trust me."

Silence answered her. Tyra glanced between Molly and Callum, then struggled to rise. "I'm awfully tired these days. I need to get back to bed."

"Can I help?" Molly asked.

"I need to do as much as I can for myself or I'll never get back on my feet. You're a sweetheart but quit trying to take care of the whole world."

Molly watched Tyra walk carefully down the short hallway, then looked at Callum.

That proved to be a mistake. At once she felt a zing of desire shoot through her, shortening her breath. No, she warned herself. No. This man wanted no one and nothing. More than once she'd wanted to help him somehow, but that was one of her problems. She couldn't help everyone, and certainly not unless they wanted it.

She looked down at the cooling tea in front of her, then dared another glance at Callum. To her surprise, he was looking straight at her, and deep in his brown eyes she thought she caught a reflection of what she felt.

You're a pastor, for heaven's sake. Cut it out. She could only imagine the repercussions if she had a relationship.

Callum rose, almost as if he sensed her reaction. "I'll say good night. Thanks for the turnovers and tea. You try to hang on to that happiness, like Tyra said. Little enough happiness comes to any of us."

Then he bundled himself up and disappeared out the door.

To walk the streets in lonely solitude again? Molly wondered. How sad. How very sad.

TUCKED WARMLY AWAY in his motel room that stank of fire, Arthur Killian was full of a great meal he'd brought from the diner across the highway, with a stack of snacks to keep him out of the cold overnight.

It was time to start hunting soon, he thought. It had been long enough that people had begun to calm down. Besides, he needed it.

Needed to punch and kick a woman around. Sort of like he'd taken care of that bitch who had been his wife. The need overcame him even now, as it had then. Only now he didn't need any excuse for his rage.

The rage existed all on its own, except for the bitch who'd ruined his marriage and helped put him in jail.

Moving on from his dinner to a packet of corn chips, he thought about it. He'd need to get his butt out in that cold soon. He'd need to look around.

And as much as he wanted to see those women while he pummeled them, maybe it was time to do it in the dark. Break his routine. Confuse everything more.

Hell, he should have picked a better time of year. Except that damn pastor had beat him up during this very season. It was too much like the best payback to do it now.

Especially when, near as he could tell, she was having a great time with all the plans the church was making for Christmas. The announcement board out in front of the place announced everything from choir rehearsals to special dinners and Christmas basket giving. Who knew what was next?

But he'd certainly get some attention taking her out in the midst of all this. In the meantime, one more. Just one more to satisfy himself.

He didn't bother to think about what he'd do after he'd finished taking his vengeance. It didn't matter.

There'd be other women. They were easy enough to come by.

Chapter Seven

In the church office, Henrietta offered Molly a stack of papers to sign and a few checks. "Although why the Junior Warden isn't doing those checks I don't know." Henrietta sniffed.

"Most people do as little as they can get away with," Molly replied. "I'm happy to do the work. What's on for the day?"

"A visit from the Senior Warden, about funding, I make no doubt. Then there's the head of the new supermarket, the one that offered the hams. The letter for him is there, acknowledging the donation, but he hinted he might have more."

"That would be welcome. So many families are hard-pressed."

"Have been for a long time," Henrietta commented. "It just seems to be getting worse with each passing year."

"Sadly." And it was sad, the hardship that kept settling over this county. Molly wished there was a thing she could do about it.

The Senior Warden, John Jason, showed up promptly on time. "Pastor," he said, his voice a little short.

Molly indicated he should take a seat. "What can I do for you, John?"

"We need more volunteers to assemble the Christmas baskets. If you could appeal for some help?"

"I suppose I can do that."

"Then there's the Altar Society."

Molly sat up a bit straighter. "You have a complaint?"

"Only that the altar linens aren't in the best of shape for Christmas. *Someone* hasn't been taking care of the darning."

Meaning Georgia, Molly thought. "You may be aware that Georgia has been dealing with a family illness. Besides, I don't think Jesus will mind a bit of fraying. He didn't exactly wear wealthy clothing himself."

"That's not the point! This church has to present itself in the best light possible. We don't want to be looking ragged. That crèche out front is, well, hardly noteworthy. I said all along we needed something in better condition."

For the first time, Molly counted to ten. "If you recall, John, it was the people of this church who brought the clothing for it. Suitable for poor shepherds, I might remind you."

John's irritation grew. "You *can* be replaced."

"At any time," Molly observed. "I never did understand why you selected me in the first place."

Henrietta spoke dryly. "I think the warden has forgotten how few applicants we had for this position given our small population and the fact that we're out of the way. Not to mention a very poor stipend. No offense to you, Pastor Molly. I personally think you're the best thing that's happened to this church in a long time. A lot of other people agree with me."

John reddened and rose. "Then do the rest of your job, Pastor."

Henrietta didn't let that pass. "You should see the pastor's schedule. I'm sure it's busier than yours. And while we're at it, ask your wife if she can make some calls on the Lathrops and Stacy Withers. It seems wrong of her not to. Those folks need more help than Pastor Molly can provide."

Molly could almost see the steam coming out of John's ears as he stomped out of the office. She stared at her secretary. "Heavens, Henrietta!"

Henrietta looked self-satisfied. "You can't say those things yourself, Pastor. But *I* can. So I said them."

"There's too little I can say," Molly admitted.

"Certainly nothing like that. It's one thing to gently scold one of the flock, another to tell off the Senior Warden. How that man got elected I will never know. I wouldn't be surprised if some palms were greased."

"Henrietta!" Molly was appalled.

"You didn't hear me say that," Henrietta said, her anger subsiding. "But I still wonder. He's never been a pleasant man."

It was a point Molly couldn't argue.

But then, hard on his heels, the Junior Warden, Daniel Alder, arrived carrying the church's books.

"I think you need to see this information, Pastor. To understand the financial problems we face. You may not be able to call for money from the pulpit, but if you have any fundraising ideas, I'd be happy to hear them. Right now we're close to running in the red."

More good news, Molly thought. But as life became more difficult around here, fewer people could afford to make offerings, let alone large ones.

"We could," said Daniel, "try to mortgage the church. The building must count something for equity."

Molly and Henrietta both gasped.

"Then come up with something better," Daniel said as he marched out.

"Good grief," Henrietta mumbled. "It never rains but it pours."

"It never snows but it's a blizzard," Molly said, causing Henrietta to laugh. "Let's put our heads together," she suggested. "Along with those supposedly troublesome ladies of the Altar Society."

"Particularly Claire," Henrietta added. "She's a smart one."

THAT EVENING, AFTER several counseling sessions in her office and a couple of in-town home visits, Molly felt worn out. Her shoulders weren't always big enough to bear the burdens of others, and sometimes she felt so helpless.

Seeking grace, she stood in front of the church, looking at the crèche and the facade of a building that had been built in the 1880s, during a brief gold rush up on Thunder Mountain. A truly magnificent construction of field stone, which, over the years, had been finished inside with smooth white walls and heavy beams. A stained-glass window had even been carted across mountains to stand behind the altar.

Amazing what faith could achieve. As a light snow started falling again, peace began to steal over her. A refreshing feeling of hope and even some renewed strength.

She had known this job wouldn't be easy, and that some days were going to be harder than others. She had prior experience, so there shouldn't have been a surprise on days like today, when grief and anger could be eased so little.

But sometimes she felt exhausted by the human misery she encountered, and sometimes she wondered if she was in the right job.

Just then, the scream of sirens from two blocks away startled her out of her self-preoccupation. Running at top speed, she raced around the church to her car parked near the parsonage. It didn't always start the first time in the cold, but this time it turned over immediately.

Moving as fast as she dared on these icy roads, she headed straight for the flashing lights.

Praying there hadn't been another attack.

CALLUM STOOD IN the circle of the police cordon, flood lamps lighting the area as bright as day. This time no lookie-loos showed up, possibly because fear had taken hold. He might be new to this area, but these people were in his care and it was killing him that he couldn't make them feel safe.

Another attack against a woman living alone. This one earlier in the night, but at a time that drove most people into their homes early because of the weather. A light snowfall again—acting like fog, it grayed out anything at a distance.

Police with flashlights circled the house for any kind of evidence. So far they hadn't even found signs of a break-in. There must have been an unlocked door.

As near as they could tell, the victim had been sitting in her living room in front of her TV when the attack occurred. Light again. Always in some light.

"Loretta Sanchez," said Guy Redwing, who approached him. "Older than the rest. Medics say it's not looking too good for her. Man must have got carried away."

Anger. This perp must be overflowing with anger. Nothing personal in these crimes as far as anyone could tell. Just fury.

"He wants to see what he's doing," Callum said. Randy Webster, another deputy, approached. A stubby man who didn't seem to be able to get rid of his beard shadow, he crunched his way across layers of snow.

"Detective? Medics think he broke her hands before the rest of it."

"God in heaven," Callum muttered. The cruelty, the pain. No justification. None. This had gone a step further than the others. "Listen, I don't care if the troops need magnifying glasses. Find me something besides smeared Bigfoot tracks in that snow."

Then, hearing tires crunch in the snow at the edge of the road, he turned to see Molly pulling up in her aging Taurus. Great. Now *she* would have nightmares tonight, too. Surely this news could have waited for morning.

Damn it all to hell. He tried so hard not to get emotionally involved in cases, but emotional distance was escaping him this time. Not good for his clarity of thought. Another reason he'd left Boston.

Molly emerged from her car to stand right behind the cordon. Reluctantly, he went to her.

"No point hanging out here," he told her flatly. "Ms. Sanchez is about to leave for the hospital and then we're getting down to the nitty-gritty inside. Nothing for you to do to help."

Molly bit her lower lip. "It's early. How was she found?"

"She managed to press the autodialer on her phone. Probably her last conscious act. Now get back to your church. Hold a vigil or something. This woman is going to need every prayer she can get."

Callum turned and went back to work, but he swore he could feel Molly's horrified gaze on his back. Nothing she could do about this, either. He pounded one gloved fist into the palm of the other, then forced himself to draw deep breaths.

A clear head. He *had* to keep a clear head.

BACK AT THE CHURCH, Molly found a few members of her congregation ahead of her. Henrietta had unlocked the doors and more than a dozen men and women sat in the pews, heads bowed, while John Jason read comforting passages from the Bible.

Molly walked slowly up the aisle, removing her jacket and gloves, revealing her clerical shirt and slacks. When she reached the front, she nodded to John then headed for the sacristy. Once there, she dumped her boots in favor of black flats. Then she donned a white ankle-length alb. Over it she wore her purple stole.

When she stepped out into the chancel, she discovered that the group in the pews had grown significantly. John had fallen silent, and the Bible was still open before him on the lectern. He saw her and nodded before stepping down to join the crowd.

Then she stood in the middle of the chancel, looking out at worried, hopeful faces. They must have heard about Loretta Sanchez and had come here for answers and comfort.

Neither of which Molly had to offer. She might be the pastor, but as so often happened, there were no easy answers that didn't sound trite. There was only one place to find a true answer, and all these people knew it.

Finally, she spoke. "We are here to pray for our sister Loretta Sanchez, to pray that she will recover swiftly from her injuries. We are here to pray for Mabel Blix, who is even now in rehabilitation. We are here to pray for Tyra Lansing, who, thanks be, is on the mend. We are here to pray for the police, that they will be swift in finding the criminal so that our women can feel safe in their homes again."

She paused and drew a breath. "We are called to remember that we do not walk alone, even in the darkest nights. At times like these, that can be hard to remember, but *we never walk alone*."

With her hands folded, she looked out across the growing sea of faces and saw Callum McCloud standing at the very back of the narthex. Was he listening? Did he care?

Then she spread her arms wide, encompassing the group and inviting them to pray. A lovely thing happened then. A man stood and offered a memory of Loretta chasing his kids around the yard while they played Frisbee. Another woman recalled how Loretta had taught her how to make piecrust. Another spoke of Tyra and her free tutoring that had helped many children. One after another, many offered memories that were all good, that lightened the room.

Then, started by a single strong baritone, people began to sing "The First Noel," followed by "Away in a Manger."

Christmas tiptoed into the church.

CALLUM HAD FELT Christmas tiptoeing into that church, too, but he didn't need it. It wasn't useful, and that smarmy stuff might cloud his thinking. Although he had to admit that Molly had looked good standing up there, like an angel come to earth. She certainly appeared to belong there.

At that moment, he'd been more certain that Molly belonged in her chosen career than he belonged in his. The night's searches had turned up nothing. On the earlier cases, daytime hadn't proved any better. All they had were some messy bootprints and one lousy partial fingerprint that had come from a faucet, which could have come from anyone who had entered Mabel Blix's house. Certainly no word from AFIS.

And now the guy was changing it up, coming earlier in the night, when his risks were higher. He was at least somewhat adaptable, which made the situation all that much worse from Callum's perspective.

Usually cases were surprisingly easy to solve. Mastermind criminals almost never existed and those who tried to get away with crimes always seemed to screw up somehow. Usually by talking too much to a friend, just a little bragging to the less than trustworthy. Other things gave them away, too. Things they never thought about until too late. Or maybe never got at all.

"No man is an island," to quote Donne, but especially not when it came to crime. There was always a trail somewhere, always a clue. It was Callum's job to find it.

A little more patience, he counseled himself. Just a little more. They hadn't finished doing up the forensics on the Sanchez scene, for one thing. And the cataloguing of Loretta Sanchez's wounds, to determine how she had been struck, was only about to begin. Looking for a weapon. Still hadn't found one.

Although Callum had the suspicion that there was no weapon. This creep was a hands-and-feet sort of guy. Nothing between him and the pain he inflicted.

Callum sometimes wondered if there were degrees of evil. He wondered if Molly could answer that one.

He checked in at the office only to find no calls had come over the tip line. Great. You'd think that by now people in this small town would be keeping eagle eyes out. Maybe even breaking out binoculars and old telescopes from the attic.

But then, who'd want to be leaving their curtains open between the cold and all that was going wrong around them?

Wandering around in the cold didn't seem to be helping his thought processes any, so he turned to walk back to his dismal rental. He promised himself that if he stayed here a year, he'd find better digs.

Truth was, he didn't care.

He was passing by the church once again when he caught a glimpse of light coming from the parsonage at the rear. Damn, Molly. She knew the warnings.

Annoyed, he stomped around to the back and banged on the door. She opened it, wrapped in a red bathrobe, looking startled. "Callum! Did something more happen?"

He couldn't keep the edge out of his voice. "No more than already has. What are you doing with your lights on?"

She was clearly taken aback. "I was just…"

"Is Tyra here with you? Tell me you're not alone."

"Tyra wanted to go home tonight."

"So she's gone?" He felt his frown deepen into a dark, unpleasant expression. "Turn those lights out, now. One mess tonight is enough! You think I want to be called here to find *you* a bloody mess? Or do you think your damn prayers are all the protection you need?"

She studied him, her face sad, her mossy green eyes soft. Then, quietly, she said, "Come in, Callum."

"And ding your reputation?" His laugh bordered on the bitter.

"Callum, please come in. It's cold out there."

Angrily, he stomped inside and nearly slammed the door behind him. "Do you ever take orders? Keeping yourself safe is important."

"So is taking care of my duties. It's Christmas. I have a lot I want to do to make this special for everyone. Except you, apparently. Take a seat in the kitchen. I just made coffee."

"At this time of night?"

"I'm plagued with insomnia sometimes. This is apparently one of those nights. I wouldn't mind some company."

He wasn't feeling like company as he tossed aside his jacket and gloves and pulled out a chair, sitting on it with a thud. Through his anger, a thought twisted its way to awareness. What the hell was he doing *here*?

Molly poured two cups of coffee. "Any word on Loretta's condition?"

"No. Except that she was beaten worse than the others. In short, she's in more danger. They're trying to stabilize her."

Molly sat, looking sad enough to cry. "My God," she whispered. "Oh, poor Loretta."

"Make sure it's not *poor Molly* next."

She shook her head, staring down into her cup, her silence possibly saying more than any words she could have spoken.

"I saw your little service at the church," he said finally. "I suppose you all think that will make anything better."

She looked up, her eyes snapping fire. "How could you possibly know that it doesn't?"

He couldn't, obviously. His anger was beginning to seep away and he didn't feel like getting into an argument with her about faith or the lack thereof.

But he still had something to say. "I hate Christmas. I hate it with a passion."

She moved sharply, tilting her head. "Why?"

"Because two weeks before Christmas I came home to find my wife dead. She'd been decorating the Christmas tree, as excited about it as any kid. I'll never forget that morning. She asked me to pick up some candy canes on the way home. Except I wish I'd never had to come home."

Molly reached across the table to touch one of his clenched fists. "I'm so sorry."

"Home invasion," he said shortly. "They caught the perps but it didn't matter. Angela was still dead. I hate Christmas, and this one, with all that's going on, is making me look into the maw of that horror again. Christmas? My worst nightmare."

Molly nodded gently, her hand tightening just a little on his. "I wish I could help."

"You're the pastor," he said, more bitterness creeping into his voice. "You ought to have the answer."

"I have as many questions as anyone, Callum. The only answer I have is faith."

He snorted. "Got any to share?"

Again she shook her head, just a little. "The thing people often misunderstand about faith is that it's not a choice. I believe, as do others, that it springs from a grace given by God. It's possible to ignore that grace, but it's not a choice to receive it."

He felt something internal shift a bit. "So what do you do about atheists?"

"Nothing. Welcome them as fellow travelers in a difficult world. They have as much right to their doubts and their questions as anyone else."

"You don't see them as sinners?"

"How could I?" She offered a small smile. "Faith springs from grace, remember? Besides, it's not my place to judge."

Callum sat back, sipping his coffee at last, his anger unwinding slowly. "You're unique."

"I hope not. In fact, I'm quite sure I'm not. These ideas are hardly original. They might be more accurately called interpretations, but they're interpretations I accept because they resound in me."

Well, he could understand that part. And here he was occupying her tiny kitchen at midnight, drinking her coffee, visiting her when she might get in trouble for it.

"I should go," he said. "It's late—I wouldn't want to cause you any gossip." Although he wondered how he possibly could after having seen her on the steps of the chancel tonight. The image of her with her arms outspread and her sleeves draping down from them almost like wings would stay with him forever. It must stay with everyone who saw it. An angel come to earth.

She didn't object, but as he turned one last time to look at her, he saw something he never would have imagined from all the strength she had shown tonight.

Overwhelming sorrow. A woman who looked as if she could bear no more. God!

Without thought, he swept her into his arms, into the tightest, most reassuring hug he could give her. This woman could be worn down, too. Could be overburdened.

"Molly," he said roughly. "We'll get to the bottom of this. But don't let it kill you. Don't wear yourself out."

She trembled slightly, in a way that whispered her need for strength to lean on. "I know," she said finally. "And I have to take care of my people as much as possible. This is *Advent*, for the love of God! A time of hope and joy and anticipation, and I'm not going to let this bum steal it from everyone!"

Her voice had grown stronger as she spoke against his chest, and she was no longer trembling like a leaf. He continued, however, to hold her close. "Much as I hate Christmas, I'll help in any way I can, Molly. Promise. Just let me know."

A sniffle issued from her, sounding precariously like a tear had escaped. "Come over tomorrow whenever you can and help me hang the last of those gingerbread men."

"And then?"

"Ask me then." She drew back and raised a hand

to touch his cheek gently. "Thank you, Callum. From the bottom of my heart."

"Just turn off these damn lights. Work by a candle if you have to."

Then, grabbing his jacket, he disappeared again into the winter night.

WHAT AN INTERESTING MAN, she thought as the emptiness of the parsonage closed around her once again. She wished she could call Tyra to see how she was doing, but it was far too late and she didn't want to disturb her friend's sleep.

Her homily for Sunday waited on her small desk in her study, but she felt she was going to have to throw it out and start over after what had happened to Loretta Sanchez. Loretta was one of those quiet women, always with a ready smile, but generally so quiet she could pass unnoticed a lot of the time. Regardless, she was always there when any type of help was needed.

Somehow she had to address these tragedies without killing the holiday, especially for the children.

At last she dressed for the outdoors and stepped into air so cold that it threatened to take her breath away. Pulling up her fur-edged snorkel hood so there was only a small area open to the outside world, so that her breath would warm her face and keep it from freezing, she locked the door of the parsonage for the first time since she'd moved here, and walked around to the church's side door.

For a while, heedless of the chill that crept slowly through her outerwear, she stood looking up at the night sky, full of questions and hearing no answers, except possibly an internal quiet. Then she turned toward the church.

To conserve energy, the office wasn't a whole lot warmer than the outdoors, or so it felt. Disregarding the frigid temperature, Molly unzipped her jacket and stepped into the nave, pausing to light a candle before taking a seat in the front pew.

Tomorrow, she knew, was going to be a very busy day regardless of what might be on her calendar. Word would spread and her office would be full of people who needed only the comfort of being able to talk about what had happened.

And sometimes that was enough, just enough, to be able to talk freely without getting into an argument or dispute. Or find one's fears too closely echoed. People needed calming, not ramping up.

Although she was perilously close to ramping up herself. Rage, such as she had rarely felt, was eating at her. Memories of her National Guard days returned, bringing with them those times when violence had been willfully practiced.

A violence that now made her clench her fists. She had chosen this calling, but right now she wished she hadn't. She frankly wanted to smash someone or something.

In the pleasant warmth of one lousy motel room, Arthur Killian pigged out on French fries with a couple of sticky buns awaiting him on the small end table.

That diner guy, Hasty, didn't mind filling a thermos with hot coffee, either. If he wanted to, he could run back and get a refill, no charge.

An odd way to run a business, Arthur thought.

But his thoughts didn't stay on his food or Hasty's coffee. No, they returned to the night's triumph. Man, had he enjoyed battering that woman. Part of him hoped she never woke up again.

But Arthur Killian didn't have any taste for murder. It was the easy way out for the victim, and Killian wasn't a guy who wanted to miss any sadistic pleasure he could find.

So he guessed he'd messed up tonight. But it had felt so good to kick and punch that mewling woman. Too good to stop until she fell silent. A beating he could really sink his teeth into.

In fact, he *had* bitten her, just to taste her fear, in a way he'd never done before. He liked it. Liked it enough that he was going to do it to that Molly Canton when he got around to her.

But that had to wait. He was pretty sure the cops were looking for him, so he should maybe wait until they thought the attacks had stopped. He sure was comfortable enough here. He could wait. Even if he wasn't good at it.

Tomorrow night, he decided, he'd break some windows. Keep the cops on two tracks, not just one. Divide and conquer, that was the thing. Maybe take some crap out of one of those stores. Like that jewelry store. He could take enough from there to make them think they had some robbers at work.

He liked that idea and gulped some more fries. Those sticky buns were smelling better by the moment. He didn't have to wait long for them.

Chapter Eight

Callum was walking the streets again, hating himself and feeling like a total failure. It was his job to find this bastard, his job to protect this whole damn town. And he was failing in a way he couldn't excuse in himself.

He avoided looking up at the cheerful holiday decorations that hung from nearly every lamppost. He avoided looking at the decorations that were filling yards and hanging from houses. All tinsel and glitter without meaning. All it did was burn energy unnecessarily.

And it sure didn't improve his mood any.

One new clue. He had one new clue, about as useless as the fingerprint. Boot marks stamped into the body of poor Loretta Sanchez. Partial prints of those soles, but at least another clue, better than the Bigfoot prints in the snow.

As for Ms. Sanchez, she'd had to be airlifted to a larger hospital in Cheyenne. Things were not looking good for her.

Failure. A woman sitting in front of her TV in the evening. She should have been as safe as a baby in its crib. She shouldn't have had a thing to fear in this entire world.

He ground his teeth, then caught himself. How many times had his dentist warned him he was grinding his way into dentures?

Not that he cared now if he became toothless in the next week. Whatever.

He'd been avoiding walking near the church for a couple of days, despite Molly's invitation to help hang gingerbread men on the tree. He wasn't the type for that kind of cuteness.

But he was avoiding the church for another reason: Molly. He wanted to see her. Very much wanted to see her. No good. Not for her, especially, but bad in general. He was a husk of a man, and she'd find nothing worth risking her reputation for.

Before he realized what his feet were doing, he walked toward Good Shepherd. At first he didn't pay much attention, was mostly lost in thought and his steady strides, but then a bright field of red brought him to a dead stop.

By the side of the church was an old cemetery, and some of those teetering stones were likely as old as the church itself. But the stones didn't catch his attention.

No, at every single stone stood a bright red poinsettia. At first he could hardly believe his eyes, but then he felt his chest tighten, and he drew a deep breath, trying to ease the unwanted feeling.

Someone had done that. Someone had gone to all the trouble and expense to make those graves beautiful, to make sure they were remembered. Who did a thing like that?

Swallowing hard, a need he hadn't felt since the year after his wife died, he tried to move on, tried not to feel touched by this act. But he remained frozen, looking at that extensive field of red, trying to absorb everything it meant.

It tried to reach every part of him that had somehow been cut out.

Eventually, a movement in the corner of his eye caught his attention and he turned quickly, instinctively.

There was no mistaking that red parka amid a heap of snow. Molly. What the devil?

His legs unlocked and he walked her way, making sure to call her name so she wouldn't be startled.

She'd been bent over, but now she straightened and smiled. "Hi, Callum. You're out late."

"So are you. Insomnia?"

"It can be useful."

"What are you doing?"

"Trying to build a snowman for the kids. I'd like it to look like the kind that are always pictured in movies and cartoons, but I'm not sure I'm succeeding."

A snowman for the kids? For the second time in a half hour, surprise shook him. "Why are you building it? Don't they make their own?" He was quite sure he'd seen a couple of formless lumps in yards he'd passed.

"The snow is the problem." She bent and scooped up a couple of handfuls, then threw a snowball at him.

He ducked, but before it could hit him, there was nothing left.

"See?" she said. "Too dry. It won't stick together."

He nodded. "So how are you getting around it?" Because her snowman looked as if it already had a head on it.

"Magic." Then she giggled. "Naw, not magic. The snow in the snowbanks is a lot firmer and stickier because of the pressure the plows put on it, so I'm using that."

"Great idea."

"So far it's working. But good mommas and daddies don't let their youngsters get into these banks so they don't have access to the packed stuff. Too many dangers. I, on the other hand, don't have to report to parents."

In spite of himself, he felt his face cracking into the weirdest expression he'd experienced in a very long time: a smile.

"Ah," Molly said. "So you *can* smile. I was beginning to wonder if you had nerve damage."

His smile grew and he scooped some snow from the nearest bank and patted it into a ball. "You ready, Pastor?"

"Nothing like a good snowball fight. Just look out for pebbles in that snow."

She had a good point, and, of course, that was one of the reasons parents didn't want kids playing with that snow. He lobbed his snowball to one side of her.

She tilted her head. "Chicken?" she asked.

"I'm not in the habit of bruising angels."

He had no idea where those words had come from but he didn't care. It had slipped out and he kind of liked the way her expression became embarrassed. He couldn't tell if she flushed because the cold had nipped her cheeks.

"I'm no angel," she said swiftly.

"Good, because perfection is boring."

That pulled a laugh from her—a rolling laugh that brought that stupid smile to his face again.

"Come on," she said. "I'm freezing. I want a hot drink, and then you can help me pick out a carrot, some buttons and a scarf for Snowy here."

"What, no hat?"

She replied dryly, "I don't think a balaclava would cut it."

THE INSIDE OF her kitchen was warm, possibly the warmest room in her small house. It was also redolent of vanilla and chocolate, and some other scents he couldn't identify. The counters and the table were full of cupcakes.

He looked around. "Have you been going crazy or something?"

She grinned. "Big events tomorrow. Kids will spend the morning finishing their decorations, then the children's choir will have a rehearsal followed by a practice by our Wassailers."

"Wassailers?" he asked.

"And old Norse term for a group of people who go around the neighborhoods singing Christmas carols.

We have two groups but they practice together. And in the evening, the full choir will rehearse."

"That's a lot of singing," he remarked, not knowing what else to say.

"It's beautiful. Let me make a little room so we can have something hot to drink. I was beginning to feel frozen to the bone."

"Are you baking cupcakes for everyone?"

"Oh, no," she laughed. "Others are baking, too. These won't last long, not with so many people."

She made cocoa for him but tea for herself.

"Calories again?" he asked.

"A little caution. I can put on five pounds in a snap."

He just shook his head. "As hard as you work, I'm surprised you don't have to eat like an athlete."

"Metabolism. Say, why don't you join us tomorrow?"

He merely stared at her as he sipped the cocoa.

"Oh, come on," she persisted. "It's not only fun, but you can catch up on all the gossip."

The gossip part appealed to him. Maybe he'd overhear something useful. "Don't you folks disapprove of gossip?"

"Of course, we do, especially if it's malicious. It happens, anyway. What's more important is that you'll get to know more of the local people. It'd help your work, I'm sure, not to always be the stranger around here."

That was true. Very true. Once people got to know you, they started to trust you and might very well pass along information they wouldn't have otherwise. But all those Christmassy activities?

Oh, buck up, Callum, he told himself. Some things couldn't be avoided forever. Or hidden from.

"I know you have a problem with this season," Molly continued gently. "But Advent is a time of hope, of love, and the anticipation of a miracle."

He didn't believe in miracles, but for some reason her words didn't put him off. Whether he agreed with her or not, he liked her attitude.

"Maybe I will," he answered, making no promises.

"Good. The kids will start with the decorations about nine. Plenty of parents will be there."

He nodded. "Okay."

"Now," she said, "let's find that carrot and those buttons. I even think I have an old scarf I've used before." She cocked an amused eyebrow his way. "I'm not a very good knitter."

MOLLY WAS CONTENT with Callum's sort-of agreement to come to the festivities tomorrow. A minor victory, perhaps.

She had a stack of large, round black buttons she kept on hand for snowmen and who knew what else. They came in handy. The carrot was easy to find. The scarf was buried in a box of odds and ends from the knitting project she'd started so hopefully, only to discover she didn't have the hands for it.

A short while later the snowman was decorated and she stood back to admire it. "The kids will love it in the morning."

"I'm sure they will."

Then Callum turned away. "See you, Molly."

Yeah, but when? Still content, Molly returned to the parsonage, remembering those two genuine smiles he'd let slip past his guard.

He was a remarkably attractive man. Gorgeous. He made her tingle. She yanked her thoughts away from *that* however. Not to be.

But those smiles were also a good sign. Maybe the man was softening up a bit.

Humming quietly, she went to her little office to work on her homily for Sunday. She might be cheating a bit, but she wasn't above cannibalizing her homilies from earlier years. There was only one way to say some things.

FOR HIS PART, Callum headed back to his own place trying not to think about Molly. That woman was getting under his skin and he wasn't sure he liked that. One thing he could say—her cheerful nature didn't seem to be forced. It was part of her.

At home, such as it was, weariness began to catch up with him. He was sure he'd only just closed his eyes when his cell phone rang.

The jewelry store had been burgled.

Chapter Nine

The predawn hours had grown cold enough and windy enough to cut through Callum's winter clothing. He wondered if he ought to ask someone around here for some advice about better gear.

But it was a mere passing thought. His eyes felt gritty, whether from lack of sleep or the cold he didn't know or care. Once again, standing in the middle of a police cordon with red, white and blue lights flashing off buildings and snow, he stared at the broken window and waited for the techs to gather evidence. Shortly they'd let him in to walk through a cleared area.

In the meantime, he began to wonder if he'd brought a crime wave to this town. From the talk at the office, they weren't used to having more than one major crime to deal with at a time. Now they had two, plus the vandalism.

Randy Webster approached him. "Ken Yost is on his way over."

"Yost?"

"The owner of the jewelry store."

"Good. That was my first question. You're right on top of it, Randy."

Randy shrugged. "No way else to know what was taken. From what I saw when we answered the alarm, a lot of display cases had been broken into."

Callum nodded, growing colder and more impatient by the minute. This was different than the earlier window breakings, which had seemed like mere vandalism—bad enough but not requiring the cavalry.

This was different. Breaking and entering. Probably grand theft. Either the original miscreants had upped their game or they had yet another perp running around.

God, he wouldn't have thought this place could have so much action all at once. Hell, he'd come here to escape this kind of constant activity, not to dive into it again.

But here he was, freezing his butt off, gloved hands shoved deep into jacket pockets and…well, Christmas slowly sucking him in, thanks to one enchanting lady at Good Shepherd Church. The whole nightmare he'd wanted to shake off.

"Randy?"

"Yo?"

"How does this town support a jewelry store?"

"Get used to Wyoming, Cal. People are spread out everywhere and there's only slightly more than six hundred thousand people in the state. This town is big compared to most. So a jewelry store can make it because folks come in from all over. Hell, that's how this whole town survives right now."

"*Survive* is evidently a good word for it."

Randy grimaced. "At least we are."

"That wasn't a criticism."

"Didn't think it was." Randy turned, looking toward the store. "A good target. Better than Freitag's, unless you want clothing and toys. The bakery, too. You wouldn't bother breaking in there unless you were damn hungry."

"And no money gone from the tills." Of course not. As far as they'd been able to discover, the windows had been broken but there'd been no entry. Strange, he thought, looking at the jewelry store. This one at least made some sense. The others seemed more like hijinks. The kind of thing bored kids might get up to.

He stifled a sigh, waiting for entry and for Mr. Yost to fill out the picture. And wishing for a thermos of Molly's excellent cocoa.

Lights came on in a storefront down the street. Maude's diner, which he'd learned was the local name for the café. Early to be starting work, he thought, but maybe not. He'd been here long enough to learn that Maude had a huge breakfast crowd. Mostly older people in the early hours, but older people tended to wake earlier.

Maybe he should spend more time in there. It was probably a hotbed of local gossip and knowledge.

He was still waiting for entry, wondering which part of him was going to get frostbite, when a heavyset woman, wrapped as if she was ready for a weekend at the north pole, came hurrying down the street. She stood at the edge of the cordon.

Then she called out. "Randy? Guy? If you can get away ten minutes, I got hot coffee for all of you. Can't carry it all myself."

Randy and Guy Redwing both looked at him and Callum nodded. Why not? They all needed some warmth and it didn't seem as if they were going to get inside very soon.

He walked over to Maude before she swept away with the two deputies in tow. "Maude?"

She turned to eye him. "McCloud, right?"

"Callum is fine. I was wondering if I could use your restaurant for a witness interview."

She barked out a laugh. "Wouldn't want Ken Yost freezing to death. His night is bad enough already. Come along when you're ready. I'll keep Ken as calm as I can until you get here."

"Thanks."

She looked him up and down. "Get you some better clothes, Detective. Start with some long johns."

Evidently he *did* need advice.

The coffee showed up in short order—tall, insulated cups of it—and was passed around to everyone who was freezing on this damn street.

At last, one of the techies emerged through the door and waved to him. Again a pathway had been laid out inside—the safe places to go. Other techs kept at it. Callum doubted he'd ever have the patience they showed, or their eye for minuscule details.

The rooms were all lit up, as bright as day, causing him to blink a few times. Walking slowly along the marked path, he unzipped his parka enough to pull out a pen and his notebook. As if his fingers wanted to work.

A smash-and-grab if ever he'd seen one. Every case had been shattered. The cash register had been yanked open despite the lock.

The perp had wasted no time grabbing the easiest pickings and getting out before the cops might come in answer to a silent alarm. A hurried, poorly planned job.

He made unsteady notes as he moved through slowly, his fingers almost refusing to grip the pen. Inexpert smashing of the display cases, he thought. All broken right in one spot, leaving lots of cracked glass that still covered the contents. Leaving behind any jewelry that would have been hard to reach. Not even taking time to make more than one blow to the glass.

The cash register had probably been wrenched open by the same tool that had smashed the cases. A crowbar? Something heavy.

He spoke to one of the techs, who was kneeling by one case, dusting for fingerprints. "What type of glass?"

She looked up. "Glass. Just simple glass. Somebody needs to tell Ken Yost to go for some heavy-duty polycarbonate when he repairs all this."

Simple glass. Damn, he thought. Security consciousness in this store apparently hadn't gone beyond a silent alarm. Maybe the alarm had even seemed extreme in a place like this. Or maybe it had been required by insurance.

He finished his walk-through, looking forward to being able to walk around freely once the techs were done. Sometimes a practiced eye could see something in the bigger picture.

Randy called to tell him that Yost was in the diner. Yost wouldn't have much information to share until *he* could get in here, but he might have noticed something in the days before, if prompted to think about it.

When he entered the café, only one man was sitting there, looking as if he'd been dragged out of bed and hadn't even brushed his steel-colored hair. His narrow face was drawn, pale. He looked up immediately. "Detective?"

"Callum McCloud, and you're Mr. Yost?"

The man nodded. Callum pulled out a chair to face him and before he said another thing, Maude slapped another tall coffee in front of him. Thank God.

"How bad is it?" Yost asked.

"I can't say in detail until you look everything over, but it's bad. Every display case has been smashed, but each one still has some jewelry in it. Cash register has been emptied, too."

"I wish them luck with all those credit-card slips."

Yost shook his head, staring into space. Callum gave him a few minutes. The man was experiencing some level of shock.

At last. Yost shook his head again, returning to the moment. "I'll be honest—I never expected anything like this. And most of the good stuff is in a vault in the back. Did they get into that, too?"

"I don't know yet."

Yost put his head in his hands.

Callum sipped hot coffee, waiting. Then he said, "I need to ask you a few questions."

Yost looked up immediately. "Sure."

"In the last few days have you noticed anything unusual?" Hope sprang eternal, Callum thought without amusement. At this point, though, anything might help.

"No, I don't think so."

"Someone hanging around. Outside, maybe? Or browsing too long in the store? Someone you don't know?"

Yost snorted. "I don't know everyone who comes in. Lots of my customers come from quite a distance and I only see them once or twice. People *do* just come to browse, maybe thinking of future purchases or deciding whether they can afford anything."

"Okay. But give it some thought, please? Maybe someone whose browsing was different from the usual. What about outside? Was someone propping up a lamppost for too long? Or too often?"

Yost's brow furrowed. "Maybe. Let me think."

So Callum let him think. He finished his coffee and another appeared on the table in front of him. He could get to like this café.

"Yeah," Yost said finally. "There was a guy. Can't tell you much because winter clothes hide a lot."

"Give me what you got." Callum pulled out his pocket notebook and pen.

"He was tall," Yost said finally. "Lots of folks are, but I noticed him. Just a bit mind you, because I wasn't paying much attention—but once or twice I thought he looked my way. *My way.*"

Callum nodded, scribbling. At least his fingers were working again. "Anything else?"

Yost closed his eyes, started shaking his head, then said suddenly, "He was big. Broad under them clothes. Wearing a balaclava, but lots of folks do. Nothing unusual about him, really."

Except that he was big, tall and wearing a balaclava. Callum's heart raced just a bit. Tyra's description of her assailant. Could it be? Could these crimes be linked?

But how and why?

And Yost was right. A lot of men around here probably fit that description.

But some instinct insisted that Callum had just gotten a description of the same man who had attacked Tyra, and by extension, Mabel Blix and Loretta Sanchez.

Still, how did that fit with the burglary of the jewelry store? Nothing had been taken during those attacks on the women.

But Callum couldn't let go of the possibility.

Maybe the guy was getting careless?

MOLLY HAD SNAGGED a few hours of sleep but then she heard the sirens.

A light sleeper, as well as an insomniac, she rose quickly. After jamming her feet into her snow boots and yanking on her jacket, she hurried out her door to look, fearing another woman had been attacked. Her heart was racing even as the cold night struck her across the face.

In just a minute, she located the center of the bright

flashing lights and realized they were downtown. She steadied her breathing and turned to go back inside. Probably more broken windows, she thought. She thought of all the shopkeepers, most of whom she knew, facing a mess this early in the morning.

She stripped out of her jacket, kicked off her boots and wandered around her small house in her flannel pajamas, which were decorated with small rosebuds because she sometimes had a wild urge to feel feminine.

The thermostat had cooled the house for the night, though, so she pulled on her red terry robe and zipped it to her neck. That was better.

Screw it, she thought, and decided to make herself a cup of cocoa after all. Comfort and warmth, and just one cup might not appear on her hips, which to her way of thinking were a bit on the wide side.

Of course, maybe some of that feeling had come from her time in the National Guard. She'd always felt that she wasn't in quite good enough shape, although her shape hadn't kept her out, or kept her from performing as well as she needed to during highly physical activity. Still...

Sighing, she took the easy way out and made some instant cocoa. All well and good to make it from scratch when she had company, but for herself in the early hours? Nah.

It was going to be a long day, she thought as she leaned on her elbows over the steaming aromatic cup, surrounded by an array of cupcakes. She ought to put them in their carrying cases, but she could do that later and decided to let it go.

Just enjoy her cocoa. Just sit here and hope that the haze of sleep would begin to take over.

Instead of just relaxing, however, she thought about Callum. He was probably out there in this cold, surrounded by the swirling lights. Probably standing there freezing and wondering why he'd ever left Boston. A bad winter storm was headed their way, too, on Monday, and if it arrived he was going to think a whole lot more kindly of Boston.

She sipped the cocoa as soon as it cooled enough and put her chin in her hand. Boston. She'd seen plenty of photos of it and had read about the Freedom Trail. The Old North Church. The Boston Common. So many interesting things to see. She'd always hoped to visit the city. Maybe someday. It sounded like a very different world than she was used to.

She hoped Tyra would feel well enough to attend some of the festivities here in Conard City. They'd talked earlier that morning and Tyra, while speaking bracingly about how well she was recovering, had nonetheless sounded weary. Healing took a toll.

But Tyra hadn't wanted her to come over to visit. "You have your hands already full with all the Advent activities. Plus, I'm not up to playing hostess yet, and I sure as hell don't want you over here waiting on me. We can talk well enough on the phone. Period. End of discussion. I *will*, however, try to make it to the children's choir rehearsal. I love those sweet young voices. Now get back to being everyone else's pastor."

That was Tyra, all right. Sweet as could be until she started handing out orders. Then she would brook no argument.

Smiling at the memory, Molly went to make another cup of cocoa. Maybe it would show up on her *other* hip and balance her out. Ha!

The four hours of sleep she'd managed to grab earlier in the night would at least help her get through the busy day ahead. Then, if she was lucky, she could leave the adult rehearsal and come home to collapse for about twelve hours. That sounded *so* good. And with her homily nearly completed, she wouldn't even feel bad about sleeping so much.

Her bouts of insomnia were often useful, but not this morning. This morning her mind just wanted to wander and drift. A mental break.

Then she thought of Callum again and wished she hadn't because thoughts of him were so stimulating. She'd even gotten to the point of noticing how he walked, an easy stride as if he was made for it.

She liked his rangy figure, too. Long and lean, a man who carried his strength out of sight. A man who liked to walk, evidently. She'd often seen him strolling around town since his arrival, but had only occasionally seen him in a patrol vehicle. But back then she hadn't been paying much attention.

Boy, had that changed. Now she was paying too much attention.

A sigh escaped her as she nodded to feelings and desires she hadn't allowed herself since choosing this calling. Sure, it would be okay for her to be married.

But a courtship would probably start tongues wagging all the way to Cheyenne, and some people would start looking for moral slips. More reason to object to a female pastor.

The man had been in town for about three months and she'd never made one of her friendly self-introductions. Shame on her, but he certainly hadn't seemed like an approachable man.

In fact, it was almost as if he walked in a shield to hold everyone else at bay unless he had business with them.

That impression of him was gone now. She'd talked to him enough, she'd gotten a heartrending glimpse of his sorrow and now she'd seen him smile. Twice. The first time the expression had looked uncomfortable on his face, but the second time it had been easier for him.

A sad and lonely man.

At long last, she began to feel sleepy. She left the cup to deal with later and scuffed her way to bed. For once, sleep was kind.

CALLUM AND TWO uniforms had walked with Mr. Yost through his entire jewelry store while he catalogued the missing items. Callum kept track in his own pocket notebook, or PNB. The only time Yost's spirits seemed to lift a bit had been when he found his safe securely locked.

"The perp was in a hurry," Callum told him. "If he hadn't been, a lot more would be gone."

But damn, the guy looked sad. He must have put a whole lot of his life into this business. Callum could tell that his sorrow wasn't just a result of the monetary loss. The guy *must* have insurance, anyway, or he was stupid beyond belief. He'd recover financially.

But he might never recover from losing the sense of safety and trust that this break-in had thrust on him. Most people took a long time to get past it.

AT NINE, WITH the morning sunlight bright enough to hurt his eyes, Callum returned to the office. The place was full of deputies who looked absolutely exhausted.

And there, beside the coffee urns, the packets of sugar and no-cal sweeteners, stood a mound of cupcakes he recognized.

"Pastor Molly dropped them off," Guy Redwing said. "Nice lady, that one. We told her about the burglary. She was pretty upset."

"Yeah." He could imagine. Though not as upset as she'd been about the attacks on the women.

But as he looked at the clock one more time, he remembered. "I gotta run for a while. I promised to be at Good Shepherd for something or other. You guys start the paperwork, and I'll add anything I have when I get back. Okay?"

The *okay* wasn't necessary. It was their job, but he preferred not to toss around orders like some dictator.

Crap. He really did not feel like hanging out with some kids. Not right now. Not when he was so tired. But he'd half promised, and Molly had seemed so pleased that he was even considering it.

Well, he could handle it for a while. He actually liked youngsters and maybe he wouldn't fall asleep standing before the children's choir as they sang at least a song or two.

Besides, Molly was right. This was a good way to get to know people.

He rubbed the sleep from his eyes, downed three cups of the battery acid that passed for coffee in this office and snagged a cupcake. A very good cupcake, he thought, as he bit into it on the way to his police Blazer.

God, he must look like death warmed over. Didn't matter, he told himself. By now everyone would have heard about the Yost break-in and would rightly figure he'd been out there in the wee hours. If not, too bad.

It wasn't difficult to find his way to the church basement. The sound of excited piping voices guided him. When he reached the foot of the stairs, he entered a room swimming in red, green, white and silver. It was also swimming with kids who were running around or working hard at small tables, some of them with their tongues stuck out in concentration. They appeared, most of them, to be making cards out of colored paper. He saw a lot of strange-looking Santa Clauses.

Despite his fatigue and his desire to be anywhere else on the planet, he started to smile. The adults in the room began making their way to him, one at a time, as they could take their attention off kids with glue, scissors and markers for a minute or two. Molly's cupcakes held pride of place at the far end of the room, but there were also stacks of colorful Christmas cookies. Half-pint cartons of milk with straws stood on nearly every surface.

And soon, he was not only in the midst of kiddie mayhem, but also swamped by adult names he couldn't possibly remember under these circumstances. At least he always remembered faces.

Soon he was forgotten at one end of the basement, content to let the swirl continue while he watched.

At some point he noticed a little boy, maybe four, sitting alone at a small table. He had a card folded in front of him but was working on an angel, cut from a doily. He kept trying to cut more pieces from another doily, but something wasn't pleasing him. Finally he banged the scissors and said, "I can't do it!"

Nobody else seemed to notice, so Callum decided to step in. The kid looked so frustrated, and even close to tears. When he stood across the small table from the little boy, he pulled over one of those teensy chairs and sat facing the kid. His knees nearly reached his shoulders.

"Got a problem, kiddo?"

The little boy looked at him, his eyes widening. "You're the detective!"

"Sometimes, but not right now. What's your name?"

"Billy." Now the boy looked shy.

"You can call me Cal. So what's the problem?"

"I can't make the wings look right!"

Well, that did it, Callum thought, amused with himself. He'd just put himself into this up to his neck. "How do you want the wings to look?"

MOLLY CIRCULATED CONTINUOUSLY, talking with members of the congregation, talking to some she barely remembered seeing since the past Easter, and some she was sure had never entered the church. She thanked each and every parent for bringing their children to this event. That was the important thing.

She chatted about other matters as well, but she noticed uneasiness had seeped into the minds of some people. Hardly to be wondered at after the three attacks on women and all the vandalism. And now burglary. None of this was familiar to people who often didn't lock their doors. It hardly improved the enjoyment of Advent.

She talked to many of the children, too, some of them painfully shy. She didn't press them because she didn't want to make them uncomfortable.

Then she saw Callum sitting on a very small chair talking with Billy Carstairs. The two of them appeared intent on cutting a doily and comparing the pieces to an angel like the ones the children had recently made. A long night, probably because of the burglary, yet here he was where he'd almost refused to come. And he was engaged with a child.

That warmed her heart.

THE CHILDREN LEFT about an hour later, sticky from frosting, cookies and cupcakes. With the exception of a few of the youngest children who had become overtired or oversugared, the kids went out the door talking happily with their parents. Billy left with his dad, looking quite pleased with the angel he had glued to the front of the Christmas card he'd made.

Then the women of the Women's Club, a different group from the Altar Society, moved in to clean up. Women, of course. The mainstay of most churches.

Molly made a point to thank them, but she couldn't help. The children's choir rehearsal was about to begin.

Upstairs in the choir loft, the singing had begun. The members stood straight and proud as they were led by Georgia, who was the organist. Georgia seemed to have built her life around the church and also seemed quite happy about that.

Standing between rows of pews, Molly looked up at the choir, all those shiny young faces, and felt peace flow through her.

CALLUM STOOD NEAR the altar of the church, eyes on Molly. She was wearing her clerical clothing, of course—this time not only the black shirt and white collar, but also a long loose skirt that reached her ankles. In fact, he thought, that woman gave new meaning to the term "clerical garb." Somehow stylish despite the limitations.

He decided not to disturb her and leave by the side door. God, he needed some sleep. But just as he'd turned to go, the choir began to sing "Silent Night." He froze, unable to move, as his throat tightened.

In those wonderful young voices, the song was extremely poignant, and he closed his eyes, lost in listening. For the first time in two years, he felt the touch of beauty. When the last of the song trailed away, his legs unlocked and he moved swiftly toward the door.

His eyes stung suspiciously, but damned if he was going to let tears fall. Those had been reserved for Angela and they always would be.

Chapter Ten

The Conard County Archives had begun to turn over information about any locals who might have been recently released from county, state or federal prisons. It had taken them a while to do the research, but now it sat on Callum's desk while he poured over a stack of photo images that had been made from microfiche or film. The number of them surprised him, given the nature of this town, but apparently some crimes were common enough to get a prison stint or time in the county jail.

Property crimes headed the list, probably because of the difficult economic times. The second thing on the list was spousal abuse. Quite a bit of it, actually. He'd ceased to be amazed by what went on behind closed doors.

He'd never caught that nap he'd hoped for, and his eyes were burning, as if someone had taken a match to them.

No more, he decided. He had to get some rest or he'd miss something important. Some little clue that was probably buried somewhere that only needed to be found by someone with the eyes to notice it. Right now he didn't have the eyes to see much.

The frigid air was bracing, and he figured it would be just his luck to have it wake him up. Long johns? He'd have to ask about them because he was getting cold entirely too quickly.

As he walked, he absently headed toward Good Shepherd. His mind was racing in a hamster wheel, refusing to stop, because if there was one thing Callum McCloud hated, it was an unsolved problem.

He saw Molly standing in front of the church, waving to a couple who were just leaving. He decided to turn around, but it was too late. Molly caught sight of him.

"Callum!"

Without being rude, he had to stay. "Hi, Molly," he said when she came closer.

"On one of your nightly rambles?" she asked.

"Heading home for some sleep." And now trying hard not to notice how tempting she looked, even all bundled up.

"You sure look like you need it." Her smile was gentle. "How about joining me for dinner?"

Shock opened his eyes wider and put him on alert. "What?" He started thinking how logistically impossible that would be, given her profession.

"I've got a nice frozen lasagna that I left on timed bake so it should just about be ready. Plenty for two, or even three."

That sounded a whole lot better than the peanut-butter sandwich he'd make for himself.

"Come on," she said. "It's just a frozen dinner. Maybe I'll even throw in some frozen garlic bread."

Now he was fully awake, trying to make up his mind, when she took his hand and tugged gently. "Come on," she said again. "You look like hell."

Startled, he asked, "Can you use that word?"

She laughed quietly. "Oh, I can. Judiciously."

He entered the parsonage with her, feeling almost guilty. Her reputation mattered, as she'd mentioned once when they'd first met. But she didn't seem concerned now.

Her house smelled good again, redolent of lasagna. Her cottage was always filled with enticing aromas.

"Grab a seat, Callum."

She pulled the lasagna out of the oven and put it on the counter while she took half a loaf of garlic bread and popped it in. Then she set the small table.

"You don't need to do all this, Molly."

She tilted her head. "I made the lasagna, anyway. The garlic bread's a snap. And I'd have to set the table regardless."

"Do you always eat frozen dinners?"

"I often don't have time to cook for myself. When I can, I do."

"But all your baking?" That must take a lot of hours, he thought.

"That's different. That's for the church."

He guessed he could see a difference there: one of generosity.

A few minutes later, Molly sat across from him.

Lowering her head and folding her hands, she said Grace.

Boy, that took him back a long way. He murmured his "amen" at the appropriate time, then she started serving.

"The bread is for you," she told him.

"Oh, for Pete's sake, Molly, you look just fine. Far better than fine."

An instant silence filled the room. Molly didn't move a muscle. Callum felt awkward about letting that slip out and experienced a moment of gratitude that he hadn't said what he actually thought—that she was beautiful. Then he did the only thing he could think of. He put a slice of garlic bread on Molly's plate.

"Just continue to be thankful," he said, "and eat it. That's hardly going to add five pounds."

She blushed, which only made her prettier. His reactions had begun to disturb him. Since Angela's death, he'd been pretty much living in an emotional dead zone. Oh, grief and anger penetrated it, but not much else. Certainly not noticing how pretty a woman was.

"How's the case going?" Molly asked while they ate. "Or, I guess now, two cases."

The usual rule was to say something indefinite, something that revealed nothing. *We're working on it.*

But he didn't want to do that with Molly. This woman probably carried a whole ton of secrets about people and damn well knew how to keep them to herself.

"It's not going," he said bluntly. "If the evidence

got any thinner on the ground you could see the grass under it."

"Wow," she breathed, forgetting her dinner. "That must be frustrating."

"It's more than frustrating. Women may still be in danger. That's the highest priority on my list. The jewelry store burglary is bad, but not on the same level. To me, anyway."

"I wouldn't think it was, either," she said, putting down her fork.

"This all stinks to high heaven and if anyone knows anything, they're not talking. What's worse, Mr. Yost gave me the description of a man he'd seen loitering outside his store on a couple of occasions. It's similar to Ms. Lansing's description of her attacker. That makes me nervous because if it's the same guy then the attacker is still in the area."

"Dear God," Molly murmured. "But such different crimes."

He reached for another piece of the garlic bread, eating it while the hamster wheel in his head revved up again.

"*Very* different crimes," he said when he'd finished the bread. "Which makes it unlikely it's the same perp. So do we have two criminals running around at the same time? Or do we have a one-man crime wave? I don't know, but somehow I have the feeling it's one perp. Just one."

"But why?"

Callum shrugged. "There's no motive to the attacks

that I can find. The jewelry store is obvious. But if it's one guy…"

He stopped. His plate was clean and he should just thank her and get the hell out. To save her. To save himself, perhaps, although he hadn't been much interested in saving himself for a long time.

"Callum? Can you put the two pieces together?"

"It's nonsense."

"I've heard nonsense before."

One corner of his mouth lifted. "I bet you have."

"So?"

"So maybe the jewelry store was a diversion. Or the other way around. To keep us looking for different perps. To make us stretch our resources. I don't know, obviously."

"It's an interesting idea."

"Maybe it's just forcing the puzzle pieces together. Anyway, thanks for the dinner. I guess I needed food, to judge by the disappearing garlic bread."

"I liked watching that," Molly answered, smiling. "But you still look beat."

He nodded, pushing away from the table. "I can wash up."

"You can just head home and find your bed. There's hardly a thing to do."

Their eyes locked, briefly, and Callum felt heat zing through him. For just a moment he thought he saw it reflected in her mossy green eyes.

Then she practically shooed him out the door, which amused him. First she'd taken him by the hand to get him here, and now she was sending him on his way. Good-naturedly, of course. That was Molly.

But she still sent him away when he very much wished he could stay.

MOLLY CLOSED THE door behind him, looking at the dinner remains with a smile. He'd polished off the food, which meant no leftovers and that he'd left with a decently full stomach.

It seemed like the least she could do, given the difficulty of his days right now.

Sending him on his way had been the right thing to do, but she wished she hadn't needed to. She'd have loved it if he could have stayed. If they had been able to get to know each other better. If they could have followed the usual course of a man and a woman who felt drawn together.

This was one of the times she intensely disliked the collar she wore. One of the very few times.

But like any normal woman, she hungered for a man's touch. For Callum's touch. Needs within her kept threatening to overwhelm her. That was not good.

Maybe she should just keep her distance. Her nature kept wanting to help the man with his grief, so she kept reaching out, and every time she reached out she knew she was making a mistake. Her position here was precarious enough.

She forced herself to think about something else. Like the fact that Jenny Clancy was coming over to clean the parsonage on Monday so she'd better have everything ready, including the clothes that needed to go to the dry cleaner. Jenny would also do her laundry, bless her.

She would conduct two Advent services in the morning, which meant she'd better find sleep soon. She needed to be rested and on the top of her form. Her day would be devoted to her congregants and the planning of the fundraiser she'd promised to produce so John Jason and Daniel Alder could stop worrying about cash flow.

They were justified in their concern and although Callista had scolded them, telling them that fundraising wasn't the pastor's job, Molly knew that in part, at least, it *was* her job.

After putting her clothing in the hamper and donning flannel pajamas, she crawled under the covers and rested her head on the pillow. She was tired—she *would* sleep.

Then the bed betrayed her. She kept imagining Callum beside her.

"Oh, man," she said aloud. "This *has* to stop."

Good luck, her body answered.

OUTSIDE IN THE miserable cold, Arthur Killian watched the detective leave Molly Canton's little house and felt a surge of anger.

The last thing he needed between him and his prize was a guard dog. As it was, Molly was never alone except when she was inside that cottage, and even then not all the time.

But during the night she was frequently alone. Unless that damn detective started staying overnight.

He was furious but unable to do anything about it

because some guy with a snowblower started working on the walkway to the cottage.

Killian slipped away, telling himself his moment would come.

In the meantime, he decided that his move on the jewelry store had been brilliant. It sure had worked better than breaking windows. He'd enjoyed standing on that rooftop behind a chimney, watching the huge number of police officers that had turned out. As he'd hoped. Now they'd think they had someone to look for besides him.

Which went exactly according to his plan. *Divide and conquer.* He couldn't remember where he'd heard that, but he sure liked it. And he'd just accomplished it.

And the pieces of jewelry he'd taken could be fenced and he'd get some money out of it, too.

A double header. Oh, yeah.

Feeling better, he hiked his way to the truck-stop diner and ordered up a large meal while complaining that his pickup had been delayed again. "What's it with these companies?" he asked the waitress. "Like I don't have nothing better to do with my time and truck than wait around until they get their act together?"

The waitress made sounds of agreement as she served up his meal.

Yeah, he sure knew how to manage a situation.

Chapter Eleven

The morning had been exhilarating for Molly. The second Sunday in Advent and the church had been packed for both services. She hadn't expected so many until the Christmas services.

But standing in the doorway, speaking to members of her flock, she found among them a disturbing sense of worry. They had come in such large numbers at least in part because they sought some kind of reassurance in the face of the attacks and the burglary.

She hoped they'd found at least a small measure of comfort. She personally had very little to offer that would ease justifiable fears. The church offered them God, of course, but sometimes God could seem very far away and inscrutable.

She pondered that problem as she returned inside and headed for the church office, deciding that all she could do was remind them of the very real Presence in their lives, that they would never be abandoned. Even though they might think it sometimes.

Sighing, she entered the office to find Henrietta already there along with a couple who had promised to help with fundraising. Four more people were expected. Henrietta had made coffee and must have gone to the bakery for the donuts that filled a small tray.

Soon they were all gathered around the meeting table and tossing around ideas for the best way to raise funds.

"Thing is," Barney Rich said, "we did that fundraiser for the motel just recently. Add into that all the foods and gifts people want for Christmas and I think most folks are tapped out."

His wife, Marcy, agreed. "We need to set this up for late January, I think."

"Oh," said Henrietta in a foreboding voice, "won't the wardens love that."

Jesse Carlton snorted. "What do they want us to do? Pull teeth?"

That made Henrietta laugh. "Maybe we should offer that idea to them. Can't you just see their faces?"

Molly couldn't suppress a smile, though she refrained from criticizing the wardens in any way.

"Why aren't *they* here?" Barney asked. "Bunch of 'em want more money but they won't do a damn thing to help get it." He glanced at Molly. "Pardon me, Pastor."

She waved a hand. "As if I haven't heard cussing before, and I assure you, Barney, that was milder than some I've heard."

A laugh passed around the long conference table and brainstorming resumed. By the time they broke a couple of hours later, they had four ideas on the table. Several people had promised to look into the logistics.

They were off and running, as well as having something to report to the wardens.

Molly needed to attend to the stack of papers on her desk but told Henrietta to take the afternoon off. An hour later, she stepped into the church proper. Marvin was busy mopping floors and wiping the pews, and tomorrow the Altar Society, weather permitting, would come in to clean and polish the rest.

She stopped to speak to Marvin. "You aren't supposed to be here on Sunday." She smiled.

"We'll probably get that blizzard tomorrow. Wouldn't want the mess building up. With all the snow, slush has melted and gotten dirty from being walked on." He shook his head. "Won't do at all."

She returned to the parsonage, feeling her heart lightened. The rest of the day was her own unless something happened. Her afternoon of rest. Her afternoon of quiet contemplation, maybe even a good book. And a phone call with Tyra. It had been a while.

But Tyra wasn't at home. A good sign, Molly thought. She must be feeling well enough to get out for a little while. Still, she missed Tyra's voice and humor, which was always a lift.

She made a pot of tea for herself and decided to take it into the living room and settle in the Boston rocker with a good book. She'd finished her last one, even if it had taken weeks thanks to her duties, and was now ready for something fresh.

She thought of a walk to the library, which had afternoon hours on Sunday, then changed her mind. She wanted to be cozy and warm in her solitude, and the first signs of the approaching storm had begun to show. The wind had started to strengthen, sometimes gusting strongly enough to make the trees outside bend. Tomorrow promised to be a deadly day. She just hoped no one was careless of the cold.

There were plenty of books to choose from, a gift from prior pastors. She was searching the shelves for something that grabbed her attention when there was a knock at the door.

She went to open it and was surprised to see Gage Dalton standing there. "Sheriff! Is something wrong?" The frigid air began to reach her. "Come in out of the cold."

He gave his crooked smile, one that couldn't reach all the way because one side of his face was burn-scarred. Long ago he'd been an undercover DEA agent and had lost his entire family to a car bomb intended for him. He'd barely escaped himself.

"Nothing's wrong," he answered as he stepped inside and removed his cowboy hat, which was official headgear around here for the sheriff and his deputies.

"Can I offer you some tea or coffee? You must be cold, and that darn hat doesn't do a thing for your ears."

He chuckled. "It's getting time to switch to the watch cap. Or maybe past time."

He limped after her into the kitchen, accepting her offer of coffee, and claimed a chair at the table.

"So what's going on?" she asked after she started the coffee and sat with him. Her curiosity was killing her.

"Not as much as I'd like, but Callum is wearing himself out working on it. Last I saw he was neck-deep in reports about felons who've recently been released around here. It's a wonder his eyes don't fall out of his head. No, this visit is about you."

Her eyes widened and her heart skipped a beat. "About me?"

"Yup," he answered.

"Am I a suspect of some kind?"

"Not hardly."

She jumped up to get his coffee, then brought it over to him. "Then what? You're making me uneasy and you're taking your time about it."

He chuckled. "A chance to stay out of the cold. No, nothing you need to worry about. Not exactly."

"Oh, for heaven's sake, Sheriff!"

"You been here long enough to call me Gage. Anyhow, I was thinking about the security of women in this town. Then I got to thinking about you."

"Me?" This wasn't helping her at all. "You think I'm a target?"

"Not directly." He sipped his hot brew and sighed contentedly. "No, I'm thinking about it in a different way. You may think you're surrounded by good people here right next to the church, but I'm not so sure you're as safe as you think."

She didn't like the sound of that. "In what way?"

"Thanks to the parking lot and the graveyard, there are plenty of ways for someone to approach the parsonage without being seen."

"Oh." Her heart plummeted.

"I've seen enough of you, Pastor, to know that your picture is under the word *positive* in the dictionary. I want you to make sure you're protecting yourself as well as you can. You're more isolated than you think."

Isolation had never entered her head before. In her mind she was almost always surrounded by people, except for brief respites in the parsonage, and even then she knew all her neighbors. "Are you trying to frighten me?"

"Only enough to make sure you take precautions. Like turning off all your nights at night. Like locking up everything. In fact, Cal has ordered a new lock for your door. Something stronger."

"Callum has?" Molly was nearly stunned. "He didn't mention it."

"I think when he had dinner here last night he got concerned about that door of yours. I just saw it and he's right. That lock you have is little more than a latch from a century ago."

So how many people knew Callum had eaten a frozen dinner with her last night? Oh, man. All because of a generous impulse. *Mostly* generous, she added honestly. She needed to be more circumspect.

Gage continued his security dissection. "You need a stronger door, too, but I'll leave it up to the church to get you one. It's the least they can do."

Despite her surprise at all this, she could have laughed at the mental image she got of at least two wardens. Complaining about cash-flow problems, they'd never ante up to replace her door.

"I'll live with what I have," she said. "We have more important uses for money. This church isn't exactly swimming in it." Unable to resist, she added, "I hear about it all the time."

Gage chuckled and drained his coffee. "I bet you do. I know those wardens."

He shook his head at the offer of more coffee and eased himself up to his feet. "Just take all the care you can, okay?"

"I promise."

When Molly closed the door behind him, she paid close attention to the latch for the first time. He was right. Anyone could get through that. Worse, as a rule she didn't even try to lock it so her congregants could reach her.

Oh, heck. He'd left her with a sense of insecurity. She knew she could defend herself, but being caught in her sleep might well change the balance of power. Now what?

She tried to relax again with a book, but that didn't work very well. Her life seemed to have picked up some new complications.

Callum haunting her thoughts was the biggie, though.

CALLUM MANAGED A few hours of sleep, for which he was grateful. Very grateful.

Over a breakfast of oatmeal and a couple of eggs, he planned the day before him, as much as he could knowing so little. He needed some information from the crime lab about the Yost burglary. He needed some information from the medical doctors who were helping with photos and examinations of the patients, looking for something more useful than the partial boot prints they'd found on Loretta Sanchez. Scrapings from beneath her fingernails had been sent to the lab. Other small items and fibers had been as well.

There wasn't a big enough population around here to support extensive facilities, so much had been sent to the state's crime lab. Which meant inevitable delays.

The felons who'd been released recently weren't offering much, either. None of them, superficially at least, had a motive for going after those three women. The abusers, particularly, had no reason to go after anyone but their ex-spouses.

And the thieves among them didn't do smash-and-grabs. Although there was no reason to think they might not have changed their methods and approaches. Those were worth checking out.

Around ten, they held a meeting in the squad room—such as it was, being nearly the entire front of the office—and talked about their major crimes. They discussed the recently released felons, but nobody had any good ideas. Keep their ears out, listening for anything someone might say that could add to their pile of noninformation.

All the deputies present were as frustrated as Callum with the situation.

Guy Redwing expressed the general feeling. "How can anything happen in this town and no one knows about it? Even the least little things. What, are these guys ghosts?"

Callum kept silent about his own suspicion. He couldn't begin to support it, and it might only muddy the waters.

The three attacked women apparently had no connections other than that they all attended Good Shepherd Church. Their circles of friends seemed to be different, although there might be some outliers the cops didn't know about yet.

Well, there had to be, Callum thought. People who were connected to all three ladies in some other way. So far they hadn't discovered any of those connections.

Except they all knew Molly through the church. The thought made his stomach churn.

But all those women attending the same church meant they had at least passing acquaintance with other members. Maybe he should get a church roster and have his men start questioning people about whether there'd been any conflicts at the church. So far they'd focused on stronger connections. Time to get to the passing ones.

When he suggested that, no one looked happy. Good Shepherd was a smaller community in this larger community of the town, but was still a community.

"We've got to examine *everything*, no matter how far-fetched. These attacks were *personal* and they expressed rage. Time to look beyond the obvious."

As the men and women separated, Guy turned around. "Better stay inside today, Cal. Temp's going to drop to around thirty below, and it'll happen fast. The storm's already moving in. You'll feel it when you step outside."

Guy started to turn back, then said, "Oh, and don't stay here. It won't be a fun place to be stuck."

Callum looked around the room. No, it wouldn't.

"What about the patrols?" he asked.

"They're running same as usual. But they've got better gear than you have and they'll be in heated cars."

There it was again. *Learn to dress for the climate.* Damned embarrassing.

Guy spoke once more as he reached for the door. "And don't try to get gear at Freitag's right now. This storm is going to hit like an explosion. I've seen them drop the temp thirty degrees in twenty minutes. Not often, but it happens."

Thirty degrees in twenty minutes? Callum packed all the papers he could into his satchel then pulled on his outerwear.

He suspected he was about to get a lesson in the weather around here.

The instant he stepped out the door, he understood what Guy had meant. It was already colder than he'd felt here so far, and treetops had begun to sway hard. He decided he'd better take his official car. Walking was rapidly becoming dangerous.

He had just started the car and was letting the engine warm up a bit when his cell phone rang.

"Hi!" said Molly's cheerful voice.

"What's up?" he answered.

"It's going to get awfully cold today and probably through tomorrow. Anyway, wise people are staying inside. So I thought I'd invite you to the parsonage. Company is better when you're stuck inside and I *do* have a fire going on the hearth."

He should have refused. But instead, he accepted.

Couldn't stop himself. He was losing the willpower battle with that woman.

"Just park as close as you can get," she warned him. "A few people have frozen to death in the coming temperatures because they weren't properly dressed. One woman froze going to her front door from the car. Just be careful."

Properly dressed. It was coming at him from all sides. He wouldn't have believed it was possible for people to tell that with a few glances. He must look like an idiot.

He parked behind the church in a parking lot that was empty of all, save Molly's sedan. Crap. How many people were watching him take this walk? When he looked up, however, all the curtains appeared to be drawn. In the middle of the day? Or maybe against the cold?

Molly opened the door quickly and let him in. She appeared to be wearing a blanket except she could stick her hands out of it. Like a poncho.

The first thing he said was "How can everyone see I'm underdressed for this?"

A smile tilted her mouth. "Your stuff just looks too *thin*, that's all."

He stood just inside the door, refusing to move any farther. "What about your reputation?" he asked, his voice hardening just a bit. "You don't want people talking because I spent all day here. And they will. You know they will."

"They will, if they look out their windows. Anyway, it doesn't matter. If you stayed all night, that would be a different thing altogether."

What was going on here? he wondered as he shed his jacket, gloves and scarf, and followed her into the kitchen. He pulled out a chair and sat reluctantly.

"Coffee or cocoa," she asked.

"Whichever is fine by me," he answered. Then he asked, "Why did you invite me over?"

She looked squarely at him. "Because I can't stop thinking about you."

Chapter Twelve

It seemed to Callum that all the air rushed from the room. He felt a slam of shock in his chest. "Molly—" he began hoarsely.

She cut him off, reaching for some mugs. "I figure a day together will be like an inoculation. Once we become more closely acquainted, the fascination will ease somewhat." She eyed him again. "That would be better, don't you think?"

Inoculation? It might become an addiction instead. A smart man would leave now, because Molly was the one who stood to get hurt by this impulse of hers.

He wasn't that smart.

"Do you want to go in and sit near the fire?" she asked. "I checked the weather. This storm is going to take us down to deadly temperatures. A nice warm fire is just the thing."

Then she winked. "I've even got a pillow to put on the seat of that darn recliner so you don't have to be poked by that spring."

Which was how he came to be sitting on the recliner in the living room of Pastor Molly Canton, enjoying the heat from a blazing fire. The warm mug of coffee in his hand felt good, too.

Molly sat in a Boston rocker, her face growing ruddy in the glow from the fire. "I'm so blessed by my congregation," she said pleasantly. "My wood box is always full, I don't have to shovel my own walkway and the good ladies come over here to clean and do laundry for me. Most of my mortal needs are taken care of."

He nodded slowly. "What about the rest of your needs?"

He heard her draw a sharp breath. It was a couple of seconds before she answered. "I do my own grocery shopping."

Quick diversion, he thought, feeling amused.

"Anyway, I'm ready for this storm. A full refrigerator—"

"And freezer," he teased.

She laughed lightly. "Well, yes. But also a full pantry."

He finally dragged his gaze from the fire and dared to look at her. "Ready for the worst?"

"Ready not to have to go to the grocery in bad weather. Plus, finding a time to do it can be difficult."

"You must be awfully busy."

"Mostly," she answered, "but today's a wash. It'd be foolish to go out, so I canceled my home and hospital visits." She sighed. "I do so hate to do that. But me turning into a Popsicle wouldn't help anyone." She turned her head to look at him. "The full weight of the blizzard is going to be on us soon. The temperature is going to take a serious nosedive and from the speed this thing is moving, it's not going to be long before it's here."

"This must be a bad one to have folks heading for safety."

"It is. Blizzards happen, but the temperature doesn't usually sag this fast. Or this much all at once."

They sat in companionable silence as the fire crackled and danced. Mesmerizing shadows and orange light danced around the room.

After a bit, Callum asked, "What about Molly Canton. Who was she before this church?"

"Nothing exciting about my life story."

"I'd still like to know you better."

She glanced at him. "Happy childhood. I was lucky. Then, when I was in college, both my parents were killed by a drunk driver. He swerved off the road onto the sidewalk and hit four people. Sadly, my parents didn't survive."

"That's tragic. I'm sorry."

"I've grown used to it."

"Then?" he asked, prompting her.

"Well, the thing people seem to find most interesting about me is that I served in the National Guard. Did I mention it?"

"I think you may have."

When she said no more, he poked his nose further into her life. "It must have been an interesting journey from the National Guard to here."

She shrugged and smiled at him. "I think I told you, I joined the National Guard in part because I wanted to be able to help in disasters and because, much less altruistically, it helped pay for my education. The helping-in-disasters part, unfortunately, wasn't the only part."

Her face darkened, and he let her be. Unpleasant memories seemed to be plaguing her.

After a while, she shook herself. "After all that, I went to seminary, served in a few different churches as a deacon, and then I was offered this position." She turned her face his way and her voice grew dry. "I suppose I don't need to tell you how useless a woman in the clergy can be made to feel."

"I can guess." He admired Molly's determination to tough it out. She must be both stubborn and brave. But he felt sad, too, that following her dream must have cost her a lot. Yet here she was with her own church and her own flock.

"Want me to turn on the Christmas tree?" he asked when he decided he didn't want to pry any deeper.

Her head jerked a little in surprise. "I thought you hated stuff like that."

He looked at the tree and realized he didn't. Molly had managed to dig him out of his emotional grave, at least a little.

Rising, he went to turn on the tree. "It *does* look pretty," he remarked as fiber-optic lights danced with changing colors all over the tree. Then he turned and lifted his mug from the table. "I'm getting more coffee. Want some?"

She hadn't quite finished hers but nodded. "Sure. This is getting lukewarm. Thanks."

He could feel her gaze on him as he headed the short distance to the kitchen.

DURING THE FEW minutes that Callum was in the kitchen, Molly heard the wind pick up more. It was now whistling as it rounded the corners of the parsonage, reminding her that this was no ordinary blizzard. Her insulating curtains dampened the sound some, just the way they kept the heat inside. It was still afternoon, but the drapes kept the light out, too.

She thought about turning on a lamp, then decided against it. Between the fire and the Christmas tree, there was enough light to see by.

Callum returned with two steaming mugs and handed her one.

"Thanks," she said again, watching him settle into the recliner. He moved with such ease, a man comfortable in his body. She also liked that he was rangy rather than heavily muscled. And she sure liked the view when he bent over and the denim of his jeans stretched across his behind.

She could have laughed at herself. *Getting it bad, are you, girl?* as Tyra would have said. Well, yeah, but that didn't change anything.

He provided her with a good view of his behind as he bent to put another log on the fire.

"Mind if I look outside?" he asked. "It'll mean opening the door."

She laughed. "Just do it quick."

She heard the latch lift, but within thirty seconds

she heard it close again. A draft of icy air twisted around her neck.

"Okay," he said. "The snow is blowing sideways. A great day to be indoors. Plus, it feels as if it's growing a lot colder."

"I'm not surprised. It's supposed to. Anyway, it's cozy in here."

"I can't disagree. You know, your life doesn't sound as boring as you might think. Guard training is no joke."

"I can't compare it to anything else. Now what about your life?"

He didn't answer for a while, as if there were things he didn't want to say, or if he was wondering where to start.

Presently he spoke. "I don't have any parents, either. Breast cancer took my mother at an early age. My dad made it long enough to retire."

"Retire from what?"

"He was a cop, too. I never thought about doing anything else."

"But why leave Boston to come here?"

"Because it got to be too much after my wife was killed. Oh, hell, maybe it was becoming too much even before that. I saw a lot of ugly things in my career. Too many, maybe. I kept at it after Angela died, but it really began to get to me. I thought coming to a small town might help. Less violence."

"And you walked right into this. You must be feeling you didn't get away from anything at all."

"At the moment, yeah. I've been assured that will change, once we get these cases solved."

Molly felt awful for him. His new life was turning into his old one. "I guess," she said slowly, "that neither of our lives is as boring as we said."

"Maybe not." He shook his head a little as if to shake something off.

"It *will* get better around here, I promise. We have our share of crime, but nothing like this. Of course, I haven't lived here that long."

"Doesn't matter. Like I said, the people at the office are saying the same thing, and most of them have been here almost their entire lives."

"They would know."

Silence fell again except for the whistling wind.

"The snowdrifts are going be deep," Molly said.

"How so?"

"Snow around here is usually dry. You saw that when I was building the snowman. The wind will push it around until anywhere there's a quiet place, it'll fall into a drift. Some folks are going to have to shovel just to get out their front doors."

"Fun."

He looked at her again and Molly felt an electrical crackle between them. She rose suddenly, driven by a need for self-protection. Not only would it not be good for her to have a brief sexual relationship—and given that he was still grieving, that's all that it could be—but she also didn't want that. She'd never want that.

"Have you eaten since breakfast, Callum?"

"No."

"Me, neither. I'll make us some lunch. Soup and sandwich? I warn you the soup is out of a can."

He half smiled. "Like I'm going to complain? I'm no chef. Soup and I are best friends."

She returned his smile. "I'll go see what I have in the cupboard."

She headed for her pantry and found some cans of New England clam chowder. Before pulling them off the shelf, she went to look around the door into the living room. "Can I insult you with canned clam chowder?"

"Why would that insult me?"

"You're from Boston," she pointed out. "You must have eaten better chowders. Crackers instead of sandwiches?"

"Sounds perfect."

Then she left him where he was, following his own paths of memory, she was sure.

As she stirred the soup on the stove, she thought about his wife, wondering what she'd been like. Her death had obviously gutted him in some essential way. He must have loved her very much.

And it had ruined the holiday season for him. Well, at least he'd been willing to help with the snowman. And hadn't he just turned on the tree? Then there was Billy, of course. Thinking about him taking the time to help that little boy with his Christmas card touched her. Everyone else in the room had been too preoccupied to notice that Billy was having a hard time, but Callum had noticed.

A good man, she thought. A very good man.

The soup was hot, so she asked him if he'd rather eat in the kitchen or off a TV tray in the living room.

He rose and stretched. "Kitchen would be easier."

"And colder," she warned him. "No insulating curtains in here."

"The soup will make up for it."

After filling two soup bowls, she found a smaller bowl and filled it with oyster crackers. "Help yourself."

He apparently liked them because he dumped a generous handful on his soup. "Smells like home," he remarked, then looked stricken. He started to put down his spoon.

"Callum?"

He glanced at her.

"This may not be home, but you're still allowed to eat some canned soup and crackers."

After a moment, he nodded and slipped his spoon into the bowl.

Molly spoke as she lifted a spoonful of soup. "I wish I knew the secret of eating soup without it dribbling on my chin."

He surprised her with a snort of laughter. "I sure don't. I won't tell if you don't."

"Deal," she told him.

Their lunch passed pleasantly enough while she shared some of her knowledge of the town and county.

"The county is huge," she said. "There are sheriff's substations scattered around. I don't think you'll see those deputies very often. Most of the communication with the office in town is by radio. Mostly there are tiny towns scattered around the ranch land. Some as small as two or three hundred people. And the ranches go on forever, it seems. I still get awed by it."

"I haven't had much of a chance to look out there."

"When the weather gets a lot better, take a few days to scout. You'll be amazed."

"And the town?"

"Five thousand people, give or take. That makes it a large town by Wyoming standards."

"And here, I thought this place was small," he said dryly.

"Not for this state. You'll get used to it. But, anyway, most everyone knows everyone. That's why getting hooked into the grapevine might be useful for you. Most of the gossip will probably bore you, but you never know when you might pick up a tidbit."

"So how do I get hooked in?"

She had to grin. "Hang around for a while. When people get used to you, they'll start sharing."

"Are you on the grapevine?"

"I think I've made it at least partway. But given I'm the pastor, I doubt I hear most of it."

He rose and carried their dishes to the sink. "Does your job make you feel lonely sometimes?"

She was about to say *no*, then realized that wasn't strictly true. "Sometimes," she admitted. "There's a distance at times. I don't know how exactly to describe it. And I don't know how much of that feeling comes from me being female."

"I'm sorry you face that kind of prejudice."

"Hey, I got through Guard training and I wasn't

always welcomed by the men. A lot of them think it's tough-guy territory. That a woman can't measure up."

"But you did, obviously."

Her mouth twisted a bit. "Having to do twice as much as anyone else is annoying. Well, ask Tyra. She's faced a lot more of that than I have."

"That's sad, too. It's the same in the police force, you know. Female officers get too much crap and face a lot of doubt from some people. And as for Black officers…well, they must sometimes feel like they're living a nightmare. But they stick around and if you ask me, they're the toughest of the tough on the force to survive that bigotry and keep going."

"Being Black is an emotional battering. Tyra's amazing. She's had to be one of the best teachers in the high school and in the process she's gained a lot of respect. Maybe some of it grudging. The nice thing, she says, is that the kids love her."

"Hope for the world yet."

He filled the dishpan with hot soapy water, but Molly nudged him aside. "Let me," she said. "Just tell me about the cases. Any progress?"

He didn't answer immediately. Just as she was about to turn and find out if he was still there, she felt powerful arms slip around her from behind.

"Molly." His voice whispered in her ear.

She wanted to lean back into him, but warnings sounded in her head. "Callum…" Her voice sounded weak even to her.

"I understand," he murmured. "You told me. But damn it, woman, I can't stop wanting you."

She nearly melted but before she could turn into a puddle, his arms slipped away.

"You can trust me," he said in a firmer voice. "You and your reputation are safe with me. I think I should leave."

She swung around, forgetting the soapy water on her hands, and splattered it everywhere, even on Callum.

"Don't you dare leave! I don't want your corpse on my conscience!"

Again that half smile from him.

"Besides, I *do* trust you." Then she turned back to the dishpan, ignoring the way her hands trembled.

She wanted him, too, wanted to say "to hell with it all."

But she couldn't. She was too devoted to her calling.

A pastor couldn't have a fling, not if she wanted to keep her church and her flock.

ONCE AGAIN THEY sat in the living room with the twinkling tree and a hot fire.

The storm continued to blow with all the force it could muster. Molly wondered aloud if shingles would blow off her roof.

"They might," Callum answered. "Any idea how strong the wind gusts are?"

Molly hunted for the remote and turned on a flatscreen TV that she seldom used. It took her a minute to find the weather, then it popped up. It wasn't long before a crawler at the bottom of the screen began to report the unhappy news.

Temperatures in their part of Wyoming were dropping, down to about twenty-five below. The nighttime temperature was predicted to fall to minus thirty. Wind gusts were reaching sixty miles an hour.

Molly shook her head. "The cattle and sheep," she said. "This will devastate our ranchers. They can't possibly put most of their herds in shelter."

"I hadn't thought about that. It's one helluva storm. And yeah, you could lose some shingles."

She sighed. "So could a lot of other people. In fact, this storm is likely to hurt a lot of people. Want me to leave the TV on?"

"I really should go. I came in my official vehicle and it's been in the parking lot all this time."

She waved away his concern. "If anyone is nosy enough to come out into this to count cars in the parking lot, he'd be a fool." She turned to look straight at him. "Unless you're desperate to get away, then stay put."

"It's not that far to my vehicle and you—"

"Oh, stop, Callum. If I was worried about that, I wouldn't have called you. And it may not be a great distance to your car, but this wind is enough to worry about even with a higher temperature."

"The car will protect me."

"From the wind, once you're in it, but I can guarantee your heater won't even start to work before you get home. Do you want me to remind you of that story about a woman who froze to death walking from her car to her front door? You might be better-dressed than she was, but look at those jeans. You can lose a lot of heat through your thigh muscles. Want to test how fast that can become deadly?"

He settled back on the recliner. "No, Pastor."

In spite of herself, she giggled. "You're a tough nut, Callum. Seriously, don't leave because of me. If you want to leave for other reasons, be my guest. I'm not trying to hog-tie you."

"You don't need to do that," he answered, his words freighted with meaning.

She felt her cheeks heat and didn't know how to respond. Almost desperately, she jumped to her feet. "Board game? Do you like *Scrabble*?"

"Sure. That'd be great."

She pulled out a card table and he opened it in the center of the tiny living room.

"I'll get the kitchen chairs," he said while she started to spread out the game.

"Thanks, Callum. I hope you're not too good at this because I frankly stink."

"Then we should be evenly matched. I have a talent for missing double word scores and I've never made a word out of seven tiles."

Molly laughed. "Sounds like me."

She made some popcorn, his buttered and hers not. That weight thing she had bothered him. Couldn't she see that she would provide a perfect armful? Couldn't she understand that a lot of men preferred to hold a soft woman rather than a bony one?

Apparently not, and there was nothing he could do about it.

But then, Molly, being a cleric, probably never thought in those terms. Or wouldn't allow herself to.

Silly words seemed to be the name of the game with Molly laughing a lot. Callum was amused enough that rare chuckles escaped him and he even made a few bad jokes.

Then, startling them both, someone banged on the front door.

Chapter Thirteen

Molly jumped up to answer the pounding. Callum stayed behind, clearly understanding the difficulty his presence could cause her.

Molly opened the door a careful crack. Fred Wilson, one of her congregation, stood there in a snowdrift more than two feet deep. Barely twenty-one, he still had the remains of a baby face.

"Fred!" she exclaimed. "What are you doing out in this weather?"

"Truck broke down."

"Well, come in!"

"Pastor, my wife and new baby are in the car in the back parking lot. They need to get in from the cold. The baby's gonna need nursing but I don't want Martha taking off her jacket. I thought you might know where we could stay."

"You can stay here, of course. We'll go get Martha and the baby. Get back to the car so your wife doesn't start worrying you froze to death."

Fred turned at once and headed back into the whiteout.

Molly closed the door and looked at Callum. He'd risen to his feet.

"I need to grab a few blankets," Molly said. "They're in my bedroom."

He followed her at once and together they pulled down quilts from the shelf in her closet. Then they dressed quickly for the outdoors.

"Let's not get lost out there," she remarked. "I hope Fred didn't."

Stepping out the door was like stepping into an icy whirlwind. Molly felt as if she'd be knocked off her feet at any moment. Leaning slightly backward, she forced herself to stay upright, no easy thing to do with the wind hammering her back. At least there was just enough visibility to see five feet or so, which should mean they wouldn't get lost out here.

Callum, leading the way, appeared to be having slightly less trouble.

God, her cheeks felt as if they were already freezing.

Then they came around behind the church and the building partially blocked the wind. The world became a little clearer and Molly had no difficulty seeing Fred's pickup truck. It was parked right beside her car. Callum's vehicle was invisible.

"There," she said loudly, her voice almost snatched away.

"I see it."

Fred and his family were safely tucked away in his cab, out of the wind.

Callum spoke loudly. "I'll help Mom and baby get out."

She watched briefly as he carried a couple of quilts toward the passenger side of the vehicle. She hurried to Fred to hand him another.

With both doors open, the wind ripped through the passenger cabin.

"Here," she said to Fred, passing him a blanket.

When their small band gathered in front of the truck, Callum took charge. "Molly, you lead the way. Fred, you take care of your wife and baby. I'll follow behind in case anything happens."

And something *could* happen, Molly thought, with the wind blowing so hard and the snow getting so deep. She did her best to plow a trail along the path she and Callum had already followed, but their footprints were filling in fast. And looking into the wind was likely to turn her face into an ice cube. At least it was easier to walk by leaning forward.

She kept wanting to look behind to make certain everyone was there, but she was sure Callum would shout out if anything happened.

Then she reached the parsonage door and threw it open, not caring about the heat loss. They all stumbled into the warmth and Callum forced the door closed behind them. Blankets and quilts and outerwear fell all around them in a heap. Fred took his baby from Martha so she could doff her parka.

Martha was pretty, with dark hair but she looked far too young to be married with a child. Molly led her to the recliner, saw her settled and watched Fred pass the infant to her. By then she was as grateful as anyone could be for the blazing fire.

"Praise God," Martha said, visibly shivering. "It's so warm in here."

Molly spoke. "Fred, you take that rocking chair and let the fire warm you up. I'll make everyone something hot to drink. Cocoa?"

As she turned toward the kitchen, Molly remembered the table covered with the *Scrabble* game. Well, if that wasn't a dead giveaway that Callum had been here for a while. She might have groaned inwardly, but instead she smiled faintly. Maybe the time to kick over a trace or two had come. She sure as heck wasn't going to escape the speculation if Fred or Martha talked.

Shortly, Molly passed around cups of hot cocoa. "If you need to nurse," she told Martha, "just say the word and Callum and I will move to the kitchen. Okay?"

With her baby safely tucked in at her side, Martha nodded and began to sip her cocoa. "Oh, this is so good. I got so cold out there."

Molly and Callum sat in the two kitchen chairs they'd been using to play *Scrabble*.

"What happened?" Callum asked Fred.

"Dang engine overheated. You wouldn't think in this cold…" He shook his head. "I was stupid, anyway. They'd have kept Martha at the hospital, but I thought it was still clear enough to make it home. Then the engine." He spread his hands. "I'm a fool."

"I wanted to get home," Martha said. "Don't blame yourself, Fred. I kinda pushed you."

He grimaced then patted the large diaper bag Molly hadn't noticed in the heap of blankets. "At least I got the diapers."

Martha smiled at him with evident love. Then the baby started fussing and she said, "I think Andrea is hungry."

"She'll probably need a changing, too," Molly said. "Callum, let's get to the kitchen. When Andrea's done nursing I'll clear away the game to make a changing table."

"You're so kind," Martha said. "I can't thank you enough. We'll try not to put you out for too long."

"You're not putting me out at all."

CALLUM ENJOYED WATCHING Molly swing into action. Throughout her exchanges with the Wilsons, her voice had been so gentle, like a warm blanket that wrapped those around her. Callum was used to louder voices, sharp voices, angry voices. Even the voices of his best friends never sounded gentle like that.

He joined her in the kitchen on the two remaining chairs, which he'd carried back in.

She sat for a minute, drumming her fingers on the table. "I'll need to figure out what to make for dinner. This blizzard won't blow through before late tomorrow." Then she gave Callum a wry look. "No, not frozen dinners. But, man, I'm not used to cooking for so many. Well, I can figure it out."

She drummed her fingers a little longer. "They can have my bedroom. They'll need some privacy." Then she looked at him again. "Sorry, my planning must seem boring."

"Not at all," he answered truthfully. "But where will *you* sleep?"

"We'll make beds on the living-room floor. Can you handle it?"

Shock shook him. "You want me to stay the night? But—"

"Oh, forget about that. If there's going to be any talk, it started when I opened that front door. You saw what it's like out there, so you're staying here. Regardless, can you sleep on the floor?"

"Of course." Near to Molly, he probably could have slept on a bed of nails. He might have pointed out that he could probably get to his car and get home, even without the heater working, but he refrained. This situation was beginning to be fun. "Where else is there to sleep?"

"I'm beginning to wish I hadn't turned that second bedroom into an office. And the room in the addition upstairs gets way too cold in the winter, especially when there's a stiff wind."

"Maybe you should talk to the wardens about that, too."

Her face screwed up. "Yeah, right. Especially since we need some roof repairs to the church. And other things. Imagine me asking for more insulation and double-paned windows when I'm the only one living here."

He grinned at her response. "Hey, isn't this the season of giving?"

She shook her head. "Not for the parsonage, it isn't. I can just hear the scolding. Anyway, it usually doesn't matter at all. And I guess I'd better start thinking about dinner."

THEY SPENT A pleasant evening with the Wilsons in the living room by the fire. At least it remained pleasant until Fred asked about the attacks and the burglary at the jewelry store.

"How's that going?" he asked Callum. "Folks aren't really feeling safe right now."

"I'm not surprised," Callum answered. "We're working on it."

The typical police response. Information couldn't be shared with the public. Not that they had any useful information to share, Callum thought. "You hear anything that might be remotely useful? Any little thing no matter how small?"

Callum glanced at Molly. She was holding the infant to give Martha's arms a chance to rest, and her face had grown so soft. She could barely stop looking into the little sleeping face. There was a woman who wanted children, he thought. Shame she was denying herself that part of life, all to keep some misogynists from talking nasty.

He turned back to Fred, who was frowning thoughtfully.

"I don't know," the young man said.

Martha spoke. "But there's Sally at the truck-stop diner. She says there's this one trucker who's been hanging around for a while. Keeps complaining that his load isn't ready in Cheyenne. Says it's cheaper to stay here."

"That makes sense," Molly said as she handed little Andrea back to Martha, who was holding out her hands. "Madonna and Child," she remarked almost absently, then returned to her seat.

Callum put another log on the fire, keeping the room warm enough while the wind whistled outside. He made a mental note to check out that driver.

"The Christmas tree is so pretty," Martha said. "All we could afford was a teeny one with hardly any lights."

"We'll have a better one next year," Fred promised. "You'll see." He clearly meant it, too.

Callum liked the young couple. Too young, he thought, but life was probably different out here. "What do you do for a living, Fred?"

"Work road crews in the summer. And the rest of the year I'm a janitor at the elementary school." He smiled almost shyly. "I wanna be a cop."

Martha sighed. "I wish he'd get over that. Cops get killed."

"Not that many, and sure not around here."

She shook her head at her husband. "One is too many." Then she looked at Callum. "It happens, doesn't it?"

"It can," he said carefully. He didn't want to get into the middle of a marital disagreement, but he wouldn't lie.

"Have you ever been in a shootout?" Fred asked eagerly.

Oh, hell. Now he *did* want to lie, but he still couldn't. He wasn't a liar by nature. "Yes."

Martha looked at Fred. "See?"

Fred ignored her. "I bet none of the cops were killed, though."

Now how the hell did he answer that? He decided to skirt the issue. "None died."

Fred looked at Martha. "See?"

She shook her head and gave up, much to Callum's relief. None had died in those shootouts, but some had been wounded. Him among them. Just once. Once was enough and it could have been worse. Armor didn't protect every inch of the body, especially when cops were on the street. It could be different for a planned takedown, but when you got a call on duty, it wasn't the same. Chest protection wasn't always enough.

He felt Molly's gaze on him and looked at her. She didn't look any happier than Martha. Well, chalk that up as another reason not to get involved with her. Although he doubted there were many shootouts around here, if any.

But put a desperate armed man into a situation where he felt cornered and anything could happen.

It had taken a while for him to get past being wounded, and it had taken Angela a lot longer. Being a cop's wife was stressful. Callum sympathized with Martha.

But he could understand Fred, too. The job sounded exciting, but he could at least pour some cold water on that. "I hope you like paperwork, Fred. You'll spend a lot of time doing it."

"Really?"

"You ever see a cop in an empty parking lot behind a big store? He's sitting there taking care of paperwork so he doesn't have to do it when he finishes his shift. He's got his radio live, naturally, so he can answer any calls that come in, but he's busy filling out forms or tapping on a keyboard to save time."

"I didn't know that."

Callum produced a faint smile. "Now you do."

When he and Molly had gathered up blankets and spare pillows from upstairs, the young family went to the bedroom down the hallway.

As he and Molly were spreading out the blankets, she said quietly, "You've been wounded, haven't you?"

He tensed, although he kept spreading a blanket. "What makes you think that?"

She sighed. "The way you looked when you were talking to Fred. Were you wounded?"

His jaw tightened. "Yes."

Then she totally astonished him. "Me, too."

He nearly gaped. "What?"

"There are some dangers to being in the National Guard, especially when we're at war and your unit gets called up."

He sat down on the floor, hard. "Tell me."

"Not much to tell about. I was in-country for all of six weeks. Short tour to say the least."

"Being wounded sent you home?"

She nodded. When her face raised to look at him, he saw the shimmer of tears. "You wouldn't believe the horrors I saw in just that little slice of time."

"I've probably seen some of it on the job."

"Maybe so." She plopped down her pillow and wiped her face with the sleeve of her sweater. "It's over. I rarely think about it anymore."

He doubted that was true, but he wasn't going to press her and drive her further into those memories.

She decided to leave the tree on, adding its light to the firelight.

"Why leave it on?" he asked.

"Because Advent only comes once a year. Because I only get a few weeks to enjoy the beauty."

Well, that was kind of sad, he thought.

Then, when they were stretched out on their blankets, he spoke. "There's something you have to do."

"What's that?"

"Tell the wardens you need a softer floor."

Her laughter made him feel a whole lot better about everything.

OUTSIDE, STANDING in the godawful blizzard and nearly freezing off his cojones, Arthur Killian watched the steadily growing group at the parsonage. That detective had been there all day, then those other people had come.

Hell. He'd thought the blizzard would give him cover to go after Molly. No way. Anyhow, all he could think about was getting back to that damn motel room.

He also realized he'd been stupid in coming out in this mess. Cover? It might kill *him* instead.

It wasn't long before he headed back to the car he'd

"borrowed" from a distant corner of the truck-stop parking lot. Now his main need was to drive back and get to the motel alive.

Hell's bells.

Chapter Fourteen

Early in the morning, while the storm still raged outside, Molly and Martha made a breakfast of oatmeal and coffee for everyone. The baby slept blissfully in her car seat, rescued from the truck earlier by Callum.

Gathered around the small kitchen table, they conversed fitfully. While Molly usually found it easy to get to know new people, this morning she felt too groggy to manage.

Callum was right: she needed a softer floor.

With her elbows on the table, she held her mug of coffee in both hands and gazed at Callum over it. He seemed unaware, so she simply enjoyed the view.

"Can we get the weather report?" he asked.

"It's not looking good right now." As if to answer her, the wind started whistling again. "I'll turn on the TV in a few minutes."

Martha spoke. "I can't thank you enough for taking us in."

Molly smiled. "There's room at *this* inn."

That comment made both Fred and Martha smile. "I was hoping that Andrea would be born on Christmas," Martha said almost shyly. "She had her own thoughts about that."

"Evidently. I hear babies generally do. Which can sometimes drive a mother crazy when they're late."

"And worry them when they're early," Martha answered. "Andrea was early, but she's fine, thank God. And my labor was so fast. I was expecting it to take nearly a whole day, but it was only nine hours. My girlfriend said the next one would come faster so I'd better run to the hospital at the first twinge."

Molly chuckled. "I hadn't heard that."

A short while later, Fred said, "I don't even want to look out the window and see how bad it is out there."

"I'll go look," Callum said. "I'm curious."

He pulled the curtains back at two windows then returned to report, "It's still really bad. Horizontal snow. I can't imagine what's piled up in front of the door. It might be hard to get out of here."

"Jimmy will clear us out," Molly answered. "He clears the snow for the church. The whole front sidewalk, the steps, the path to my door, the parking lot. He'll get here as soon as he can. In the meantime, may I suggest we *don't* open the door? I honestly don't want to see the snow pour in if we do. Unless getting out is really urgent for some reason."

No one disagreed. Regardless of how much snow might have piled up, it was still too dangerous to go out.

But Molly couldn't help thinking of all the work she was missing. If this kept up for too long, she'd never catch up.

John Jason called. "How are you doing, Pastor?

Got all the essentials? Not that I know how we could get anything to you right now, short of using an army tank."

She laughed. "All okay here, John. I always keep extra on hand for winter weather."

Boxes and cans and a freezer full of frozen meals. A stove and heater that ran on natural gas. Even with three extra adults, they could make it two or three more days. By then, they'd be shoveled out.

"But you're okay?"

"Well," she said dryly, "I need a softer floor."

Callum suddenly grinned.

"What?" John exclaimed.

"Just joking. No, all's good here."

Right then, Andrea decided to wake up, fussing and crying. Even as Martha rose to take care of her, John's voice rose over the phone line.

"Do I hear a *baby*?"

"Yes, John, you do. The Wilsons and their newborn got caught out in the storm and they're staying with me. What did you think? That I have some dark secret?"

John practically spluttered at the other end of the phone. Callum grinned again.

"'Welcome the stranger,'" she said. For once she enjoyed stirring the man up. "I'll talk to you later. Thanks for checking on me."

Martha had disappeared to the bedroom with the baby. Fred spoke. "I'm sorry you're sleeping on the floor. We could sleep there and give you your bedroom back."

"Don't even think of it. It's good for the soul." *If*

not my hips and back. But come to think of it, the mattress on that bed wasn't great, either.

With the bedding tucked away, they set up the folding table again and the four of them played a game of *Parcheesi*.

By late afternoon, the wind's howling had lessened. Callum went to the windows again and pulled back the curtains. "Winter wonderland," he announced. "But no more horizontal snow. Easing up, I think. What about that weather on the TV?"

Molly hunted up the remote. She so rarely watched television that she couldn't remember where she'd put it this time. She finally found it tucked between books on the shelf. At least it was easy enough to use. It was also easy to find the weather. Nearly every news channel was covering the storm, and the Wyoming stations were providing the forecast, as well as the dire stories emerging from the wintry blast.

"We're lucky," Fred said as they watched.

But the news was good in that the storm would finish blowing through around midnight.

"There," Molly said with satisfaction. "Life will start returning to normal tomorrow morning. Not much longer to be stuck. I bet you two want to get home with your baby."

Fred looked sheepish. "Well, yeah."

"Of course, you do. I don't think this is the way you visualized your first couple of days after you brought Martha and Andrea home."

After they had all curled up for the night, all Molly could think about was Callum's proximity. So near, yet so far. His male aromas reached her faintly, stirring desires she didn't want or need. Making her ache with hunger. To have a man's arms around her again would be heaven.

Well, she thought, forcing herself to remember her reasons for not getting involved, at least the presence of the Wilsons would prevent any gossip about what the preacher had been doing with a man in the parsonage.

Small blessings.

IN THE MORNING, the sun returned from its vacation, brightening the sky, making the snow blindingly bright. A gorgeous, cold day. The sound of snowplows and snowblowers reached inside the parsonage, reassuring in their promise that people could soon come out and drive again to the grocery.

By 10:00 a.m., a knock sounded at her door. Molly opened it to see Jimmy standing there with snow shovel in hand. She smiled at once.

"Your path is clear, Pastor. You can get to the side door of the church now. I'm getting the snowblower next and clearing the front, then the parking lot."

"I can't thank you enough, Jimmy."

He shrugged. "Least I can do to support Good Shepherd."

It was true, he didn't get paid for doing this. He'd added this of his own accord to doing minor repairs, a job that he did get paid for, and not nearly enough in Molly's opinion. But her control over such things was minimal, if not nonexistent.

The whole darn edifice depended on willing volunteers. Then she thought of something. "The Wilsons are staying with me. Their truck was overheating. Do you know who I might get over here to fix it?"

"I'll take a look at it," Jimmy said promptly. "If I can't fix it, I'll find someone to come over here."

There weren't enough thanks in the world for this man.

Then, all too soon, Callum said, "I can probably get to the office now. Thanks for your hospitality, Molly."

CALLUM, BY NATURE a bulldog with a bone when it came to crime, was for once reluctant to return to work. He plain didn't want to leave Molly.

But serious things had happened and they couldn't wait for his attention. He wasn't surprised that AFIS was taking so long with that one partial fingerprint. They were backlogged and, worse, they didn't have fingerprints on file for every felon because not all law-enforcement agencies forwarded them.

It wasn't like TV, where the cops had a fingerprint match within hours. Nor was DNA. Those matches never got done that fast. They took time to get results, and those labs were backed-up as well.

And with all of that, finding either one at a crime scene was useless unless they could be matched with someone.

He *did* make it to the office, though, along freshly plowed streets that were nevertheless coated with thin layers of snow. He imagined the sand trucks would follow.

In the meantime, he needed to figure out how to

investigate the trucker that Sally, the waitress at the truck-stop diner, had mentioned to Fred. And he had to investigate somehow without raising the guy's suspicions. Last thing he wanted was a possible perp on the run.

Leaning back at his desk in the squad room, he folded his hands on his chest while he thought. Funny how hard it was to concentrate on the job when Molly kept popping into his thoughts.

Her good nature, her cheeriness, her warmth toward people, even her enjoyment of Christmas, were all enchanting him. Temptress.

He swallowed a smile, imagining how she might react to that word.

You think I'm Delilah or something?

Yup, that sounded like Molly.

Back to work, he told himself sternly. Women were depending on him. Now that trucker...

He leaned forward and reached for the landline, calling the truck-stop diner to ask when Sally would be on duty.

THAT TRUCKER WAS frustrated beyond words. He'd been kept from getting to Molly Canton during that blizzard, she still had those people staying with her and the likelihood he'd get a chance at her tonight was slim.

His fury was rising again, reaching a fever pitch. He *had* to get rid of it before it drove him into doing something really stupid. He wasn't good at impulse control, according to the prison psychologist, but he needed to practice it now. The patience he'd learned was strained to the max, getting ready to snap.

He had to take this anger out on something, a person or a place. Just about anything would do.

He started thinking about the possibilities open to him. Soon he thought he had one.

He rubbed his cold hands together.

That night, as always, he went to the diner for his dinner. While he was seated at the table eating, he froze in place.

The detective walked in and looked around. Killian could barely breathe. With difficulty, he stabbed his fork into a slab of meat. Then to his relief, the dick sat down and ordered coffee and a burger.

Okay. It was okay. But he couldn't completely relax.

FROM FIFTEEN FEET AWAY, Callum enjoyed his burger and coffee. But he hadn't missed the guy at the table near the back. Hadn't missed the way he'd frozen. The way he now seemed edgy, like he was ready to jump.

Maybe that was the trucker Sally had mentioned. If Callum's appearance had made the guy nervous, then he had something to hide. And Callum was pretty much sure he'd caused that attack of nerves. He'd watched enough people on the job to recognize the signs.

But what was the guy hiding? Had he stolen some candy bars from the rack near the counter? Did he have weed in his pocket or maybe a load of it being transported in his truck? Was his truck improperly tagged? Nervousness didn't mean he'd attacked those women, and if he'd hit the jewelry store, he'd have long since left town.

But it could be a lot of things. Callum watched from the side of his eye, pretending to ignore everything except his food.

The guy ate in a hurry, dropped money on the table and disappeared out the door quickly.

Okay, then.

Callum rose and snagged a waitress. "You know who I am?"

She nodded, her eyes wide. She was a middle-aged woman who'd begun dying her hair that champagne color. He glanced at her nametag. "Sally."

"Yes."

"Was that man who just left the trucker you were talking about? If so, I need a favor from you. If you wouldn't mind."

She nodded, now looking excited.

"I want you to clear that man's table with a fresh pair of your rubber gloves. Carefully. Then carry it all to the back by itself, on a tray, or in a clean bus bin by itself. I'll meet you there."

"Wow," she whispered. "Okay, you got it. I knew there was something weird about that guy."

"Maybe so."

He spoke to the owner, Hasty by name, and had no trouble getting waved to the back. The advantage of a small town. He didn't have to flash his badge to get cooperation. It sure made something like this easier.

Sally brought the bus bin to the back and stood holding it while Callum pulled out several evidence bags and his own protective gloves. Then, taking everything by the safest spot, he lifted the coffee cup into a bag, then sealed it. After that came the fork in another bag.

He stood there marking them quickly then looked at Sally.

"Remember what we just did. Remember the items I took."

She looked at the two bags and nodded.

"If that guy did something that goes to trial, you may have to testify to the link between these items and that man."

Her eyes grew until they seemed to fill her entire face. "Wow. Really?"

"Really. And it would be a big help if you'd write down the date and time somewhere so you can't forget it. In fact, write everything down. Got it?"

She nodded and pulled out her order pad and pen. "Right now. I'll keep it safe."

"Got any idea what kind of truck that guy was driving?"

"A small truck, I think. At the back of the lot because the other trucks have been moving in and out. That one just stays there. White boxy thing, not like them big rigs out there."

He favored her with a smile. "Thank you."

"No need," she answered, her voice now growing firm. "If that guy did something bad, I want to help put him away."

ARTHUR KILLIAN DECIDED it was time to move out of the motel and start eating convenience-store sandwiches and chips. That detective had made him nervous, probably more nervous than he should be, but he wasn't going to take any chances. His goal was too close and he wasn't going to leave Molly Canton behind. Not now.

No, he needed to teach her a lesson, and the need was growing. It was hammering at him.

Well, he could move the truck out of town somewhere and sleep in it. Not too far from another car he could "borrow." He'd need a car.

Satisfied, he began to pack. Once that detective drove away, Killian would move. Fast.

BACK AT THE OFFICE, Callum asked one of the techs to try to lift prints from the cup and fork and match them to the partial they'd picked up at Mabel Blix's house.

Donna Henley shook her head a bit. "The comparison would be superficial, Callum, against a partial. We can look at it here, but we'd be better off asking the state lab to make the comparison."

"I'm not opposed to sending it on, but take a look with our software, anyway. Even a little bit might tell me if this guy could be our perp. He's hanging around. If he is, it means he isn't done."

"I'm on it," Donna answered, then headed toward the back and the limited forensic lab facilities.

And that was the downside of living in a small town, Callum thought. He simply didn't have the technical equipment he'd had in Boston.

He could have become frustrated by that but he'd chosen this path and he'd just have to deal.

And stop thinking about Molly Canton. About her easy joy in even little things, like holding that baby. Damned if she hadn't looked as if she wanted her own.

Chapter Fifteen

A few hours later, Donna returned with news.

"Well, Callum, you might be in luck."

He sat straight up. "How so?"

She laid two transparent sheets in front of him on his desk. "See that little scar on the thumb? Going sideways along the side?"

His heart quickened. "Yes."

She slid one sheet over the other. "Match."

"Fantastic. Now we just have to find out who he is." Which was the whole damn problem. Knowing the prints might match wasn't enough alone. There could be any reason the guy had been in the Blix house and a defense attorney could shred this evidence.

But he *could* bring the trucker in for questioning. Amazing how many people crumbled quickly. Or couldn't resist bragging. Regardless, it was time for a little third degree.

He called the motel and asked if they'd had a trucker staying with them for a week or more. He got the guy's name—Randy Cole.

Then he grabbed a uniform to go with him and

headed out, feeling the first satisfaction he'd felt about these cases. Now he had something to work with.

Maybe.

No one answered the door when Callum knocked. "Hell," he muttered. Then he said to the uniform, Ben Staple, "I doubt he'll show up with a uniform present. Take a look around the truck-stop parking lot." He scribbled down the info he had, which wasn't much, and passed it to the deputy. "I'm gonna hang around a bit, over there." He pointed to the side of the motel entrance.

"You got it."

Staple walked across the highway and disappeared among the parked trucks, while Callum grew edgy. Had the guy flown the coop already?

Staple returned twenty minutes later. "The truck is gone, Detective. Fresh tire marks where the lot hasn't been plowed completely. They sure couldn't have plowed under it if it stayed parked. And all the other rigs are sitting there with their engines running and have been moving in and out today."

"Well, hell." What more could he say? "I don't think he's finished. We're going to need a stakeout, plain clothes. Let's go set it up." Because if the man was after another woman, then he'd come back.

Another woman. *Molly.* A mental map had grown in his head. Blix and Sanchez lived near the church. Tyra was her Molly's best friend. Little enough evidence of anything, possibly a coincidence, but his heart lurched, anyway. At night, Molly was usually all alone in the parsonage.

Then Donna came to him with the long-awaited results from AFIS. Now they knew who they were looking for.

THE WILSONS WERE STILL at Molly's because Jerry Jimmy had told them the radiator had cracked. "Old truck like that, things happen. Lew Franklin is getting one in as quick as he can. Maybe tomorrow."

Molly looked at Fred. "Where do you live? Maybe I can drive you home."

"About two miles west of town."

Molly frowned. "Any nearby neighbors?"

Fred shook his head. "We're on the edge of ranch country."

"Then you'll stay here. I can't leave you out there without any kind of transportation."

"But…"

"No *buts*," Molly said firmly. "What if your heater quits? Any kind of thing could turn into an emergency and there's no telling how long it would take for someone to get to you."

Fred stopped arguing. He eyed his wife and daughter, who were tucked up in the rocking chair. "You're right."

"I'm always right." Molly smiled. "I'm a pastor, remember?"

That made Fred laugh. Martha looked up from her absorption with her daughter. "Thank you," she said.

"It's no problem at all. I like having you here." Which was the truth. Somehow they made her cozy little house feel cozier.

But the path between the parsonage and the side door of the church had been cleared, so she supposed she ought to go over there and take care of some work.

Dang, it was cold outside, even bundled up as she was. She didn't expect Henrietta to be there, though. The woman had enough on her plate without risking her neck to drive here. With two young adopted boys and the school still closed, she couldn't leave them home, not while her husband was out of town.

The first thing she did when she settled at her desk was call Henrietta. She could hear excited boys' voices in the background.

"I hope school opens tomorrow," Henrietta said humorously. "These kids are running me ragged trying to keep them entertained."

"You have my sympathy," Molly answered, smiling into the phone. "I'm in the office. Is there anything I need to take care of today that isn't in the appointment book?" She knew that Henrietta, bless her heart, had the church calls forwarded to her home in the evening or on weekends.

"Not a thing, Pastor. I guess nobody wants to come out yet. Anyway, you'll find the appointments in the book aren't important and can be postponed."

Then Henrietta's voice grew concerned. "You shouldn't get on the roads, Pastor. Seriously. I'm hearing from my friends that the sand hasn't been spread everywhere yet, and that there's a black ice problem in places."

Well, that settled that, Molly thought. She spent some time making phone calls to the housebound, then the victims of the beatings. Loretta Sanchez was still in intensive care. Mabel Blix was at home but sounding tired. She had a friend staying with her and was fine, thank you for calling.

Then Tyra.

"Oh, hell, Molly," Tyra said. "Frankly I'm going out of my mind without school. I keep thinking of my students who live in miserable home situations, or whose families have trouble paying the bills and buying food. School is where they get fed. Where they get real care from people who actually give a damn. Where they can escape from it all for a few hours a day."

"You're breaking my heart, Tyra," Molly said honestly.

"Why? You folks at the church do a whole lot for these families." Then she gave a tired laugh. "Sheesh-Molly, you'd save the whole world if you could. And you weep that you can't. I know you."

Molly swiftly changed the subject to one that didn't embarrass her. "How are *you* doing otherwise, Tyra? That attack was nothing to sneeze at."

"Maybe not," Tyra answered forthrightly, "but you try growing up in a rough neighborhood. Been punched and kicked before."

What an awful commentary, Molly thought after she said goodbye. She stared blindly at nothing at all, until she shook herself out of her sudden mental funk. She'd be useless to everyone if she allowed herself to give way.

Then she rose and reached for the beauty and hope that made her life so blessed. Inside the church proper, she flicked switches and turned on the two Christmas trees and the strings of white lights strung from the choir loft. So beautiful.

A rack holding several rows of votive candles flickered with a few flames. She went over and lit one, then devoted herself to prayer for all the world's unfortunates.

She knew better than to blame God for the horrors. *These things result from the hard hearts of men.* People were capable of fixing all the problems of mankind.

They just refused to.

IN THE MORNING, the Wilsons went home. Molly missed them the minute they departed. Especially the baby. Those sounds and scents would be sorely missed.

Then off to the office again to catch up on work. At this time of year, there was plenty of it. Extra gatherings, extra practices, groups preparing the church with big red ribbons and enough pine boughs to scent the entire place, as well as making it pretty. A bake sale that smelled so delicious that as Molly wandered among the offerings, she figured she'd gained five pounds just from the aromas.

Then there were her usual calls to the housebound, and when she was in the office, a fair number of visitors who needed or wanted to talk with her.

It was a full life she enjoyed, for the most part.

Today had been extra busy however, and she was glad to close the parsonage door behind her and slip into old jeans and a sweatshirt. And her silly, fuzzy pink slippers with eyes on them. After all this time, they still made her grin.

A frozen meal out of the fridge, one of those low-calorie ones. She hardly cared which. Only as she was warming the oven did she glance at it long enough to see it was supposedly pasta primavera. She didn't expect it to taste like the real thing, not with all those calories missing.

But what did it matter? Better than putting on weight.

She was just about to put the frozen tray in the oven when someone knocked on her door. Wondering who might need help at this hour, she went to answer.

There stood Callum, with a large brown bag in his hand. "Let me in," he said before she could say a word. "Or you're going to freeze in your own home and I'll be standing out here ready to be your next snowman."

A laugh bubbled up from her stomach and escaped her as she quickly stepped back to open the door more.

He headed straight for the kitchen without pulling off his jacket, gloves and watch cap. He placed the bag on the table and scanned her frozen meal.

He pointed to it. "Seriously?"

"I've got to mind my intake. I've told you."

"Not every single damn day," he said forcefully. "Besides, you need enough energy to stay warm."

She put her hands on her hips, feeling a flicker of resentment. "You know, Callum, you could help me by not disparaging my diet. Respect my decisions."

He cocked an eye at her. "Okay, have your measly dinner and I'll shut up about it. But by the way?"

"Yes?"

"I *do* respect your decision. There's a big chef's salad in this bag."

She didn't even have to think about it. The frozen dinner went right back into the freezer.

Coffee and salad made a fairly good combination, Molly thought as she speared some lettuce with her fork. "Thanks so much, Callum."

"My pleasure. What, no dressing on that salad?"

She gave him a look that silenced him. But not for long.

"You know, Molly," he said, "you'd need a microscope to find many calories in those veggies. As for the ham and cheese in there, you'd need a magnifying glass."

It was true, the salad was lacking in the meats. She laughed. "Okay. But don't bug me."

He held up his hand, palm forward. "I won't." Then he pushed a thin slice of garlic bread toward her. "Croutons in their original shape, if you want them."

Oh, man, did she. Giving in, she took the slice and savored every mouthful. She could make up for her dietary sins tomorrow.

Callum, meanwhile, dug into his own dinner of a thick steak, mashed potatoes and a side of broccoli still green enough that it claimed it hadn't been overcooked.

"This salad is really good," Molly said. "A big thank-you."

He shrugged. "No biggie. Are you missing the Wilsons?"

"Actually, I am. Tiny as this cottage is, you'd think it would have felt crowded, but it didn't. Maybe I'm getting an insight into my predecessor and his many children. I often wondered how they got by in this house."

"A lot of patience and love," Callum suggested.

Molly smiled at him. "I suspect you're right."

After they'd finished eating, the trash went into the wastebasket. No washing up.

They moved to the living room, where Callum built a fresh fire. Then he sat on the recliner while Molly claimed her favorite rocking chair.

"So," said Callum presently, "we think we know who our perp is, at least the one who beat those women."

"Thank goodness!" Molly felt a strong wave of relief, thinking that no other woman would face a horrific attack. "Have you caught him?"

"Not yet. He's not local and he might have skipped town."

"Oh." Her heart fell. "But you'll get him?"

"Soon, I hope. We've got a stakeout going on at that motel. Where Fred said the waitress said he was staying."

Molly's spirits lifted again. "But how did you find out who he is?"

"We had a partial print from Mabel Blix's house, which could have been anyone, but then Sally at the truck stop helped me get a full set of prints off that trucker's utensils. They match."

"Wonderful! But why would he suddenly run?"

Callum grimaced, his face etched by firelight. His strong chin, his straight nose, his...

Molly yanked herself back. Sheesh! Next she'd be climbing all over him.

Callum, apparently unaware of her gaze, shrugged. "Might have been my fault. I went to the diner specifically to get those prints and he got real nervous. Impossible to mistake."

"Especially for an experienced detective."

"Yeah, I think he recognized me. Anyhow, not being local, I can't understand why he'd come here to do this. It doesn't make sense. It would be hard to be any more out of the way than this town. And since he's not local, why in the world would he come here when he got out of prison so recently? That's how they matched his prints, by the way." He concealed his own ugly suspicion for which he had absolutely no evidence.

Molly nodded, rocking slowly as she thought about it. "Recently out of prison? You'd think he'd have bigger things on his mind."

"You'd think."

Molly, who'd been delighted to hear they'd identified the perpetrator, thought about the strange situation. Why, indeed, would some ex-con come to Conard City? Unless he knew someone here?

She bit her lower lip, wondering if she should question Callum any further. He wasn't supposed to talk in any detail about his cases, she was sure. But the question popped out, anyway.

"Do you think he might know someone here?"

Callum nodded slowly. "The question is crossing my mind."

"But *three* women?" It didn't make any sense to her.

"That's weird, all right. Especially since this guy was convicted of several charges of spousal abuse. Not the type to commit physical mayhem on random women."

Molly froze. "Spousal abuse?"

"Serious abuse."

"What's his name?" she asked, her voice barely above a whisper.

CALLUM SAW HER stiffen and her gaze grow distant as if she was remembering something. But she'd never been married as far as he knew. There was no way she could have been a victim of marital abuse.

"Molly," he said quietly.

Her eyes drifted toward him. "Callum, what was his name?"

He broke every rule in the book, hoping to make her feel better. Instead he made it worse, saying, "Arthur Jay Killian."

She drew a shaky breath and her face drained. "Oh, my God."

Callum leaned in her direction. "Molly? Do you know him?"

"I was instrumental in helping to put him in prison."

Chapter Sixteen

Callum remained silent. Well, that would explain the connection, he thought. She knew who the guy was, and he was here now. But that didn't explain the other women unless the guy was circling in on his prey, trying to unnerve her.

Nor was it necessary to know now. That could wait until they caught the beast. His concern for Molly grew by leaps and bounds.

"Molly," he said again.

Her eyes focused on him. She was no longer lost in memory.

"What happened? With this Killian guy."

She swallowed and tightened her lips, then spoke. "He was a vicious man. Unbelievably vicious. What he did to his wife? It was almost as bad as what he did to the women here. But he did it to her more than once."

She fell silent, once again traveling a path in her memory.

"Why isn't he after his wife?" Callum asked, wondering if she might have an answer. Abusers usually went after their wives, blaming them for everything.

"I guess she got as far away under a new name as I'd hoped."

"Which leaves you."

"That would be my guess. But why the other women? Why didn't he just come after *me*?"

"You'll have to ask *him* that when we cuff him. But what's the rest of the story?"

He was intensely curious now. Wanting to hear her part in this. How could she have made this man so furious with her that he'd attack other women? What caused the long-simmering boil?

She closed her eyes. "I was in the National Guard, serving during the week-long training. I heard something down an alley and I looked. I saw a man savagely beating a woman."

"You couldn't just walk away." He had no doubt of that. It wasn't a question.

Her eyes snapped open, suddenly looking like green fire. "Of course not! I tore down that alley and tried to pull him off her. He was strong with all that rage. When he wouldn't back off, but just kept hammering her and yelling horrible things at her, I managed to turn him around enough that he got a knee in his groin."

Callum managed to smother a grin. "Then?"

"I helped the woman away. I wasn't going to leave her with him. Dang, she was a bloody, bruised mess! But she was terrified, too. She freaked when I said I'd call the police. It took me some time to coax her into the coffee shop where I was meeting some of my buddies. I didn't even have to explain to them. They formed a phalanx around her, shielding her as much as they could from the other patrons. We got her settled under my jacket and with an icy drink to help the swelling in her mouth, and I swore I was taking her to a safe house."

Callum nodded, growing even more impressed with Molly. "But no police?"

She shook her head. "Of course, police. I wasn't going to let that guy walk away. Eventually Carla— that was her name—grew less afraid. I think it helped that she was surrounded by seven men and women in uniform, all of them kind and understanding. She felt safe."

"I should think so." He began to understand more about Molly Canton. She simply couldn't walk away from someone in need even when she'd already rescued them.

"Anyway, the police took one look at her, got the information they needed and went after Killian. I gather he wasn't too hard to find. Idiot went home. The cops had given Carla the number of a women's shelter and I made her call it. I tell you, none of the people I was with were going to let her get out of it. You've never heard so much cajoling in your life."

"Good people." Very good people in a world where, as he knew all too well, people didn't want to get involved.

"We walked her down to the corner, where the car pulled up for her."

"How'd you know it was the right car?"

She smiled faintly. "They gave her a safe word."

Callum nodded. "Good thinking."

Molly sighed and looked miserable. "Well, the wheels of justice began grinding. A pile of hospital X-rays and all her excuses for them, recorded. I can't understand why no one at the hospital caught on and called the police themselves. But it was a wonder the woman was still alive."

"I can imagine. I've seen it."

"I guess you have." She shook herself. "And I had to be a witness, because I'd seen it with my own eyes. It would be my guess that's why he's here."

"Sounds like it might be. But Carla went through with the trial? That must have been hell for her."

"It's not easy to stand up against a man like that. Talk about courage! Anyway, I guess by then being in the shelter had helped strengthen her. She testified, all right. In excruciating detail. Horribly painful to listen to. But she also came to hear the verdict. Must have been a vindicating moment for her."

"Yeah." He could imagine the woman's relief—her relief at being believed. Her probable surprise that no one had believed her husband. The instant when she realized he would be gone for a long time.

"After that, people helped Carla get a new identity. She phoned to tell me that she was leaving and to thank me. And, no, I don't know how she got her new identity. I was just glad she did."

Callum had heard and seen so many stories like this it was almost blistering. And to find out that Molly had seen it happening like that? He wished he could erase her memory because she was clearly still troubled by it.

After Molly fell silent and turned to stare into the fire, Callum waited before speaking again.

"I'm sorry you had to see that, Molly."

"I've seen worse," she said tautly. "I've been to war however briefly, remember?"

When she turned her head toward him, he saw her tears glisten in the firelight.

"Why," she asked in a tremulous voice, "do people have to be so cruel? Why?"

"I wish I knew." But her tears touched him so deeply that he gave up trying to think about anything except Molly. Rising, he went to take her hands gently and tug her up from the rocker. Then he led her across the room, sat and pulled her into his lap.

"I guarantee I won't bite."

A small watery laugh escaped her, but then she turned her head into his shoulder and gave in to her tears. They dampened his shirt but he could only feel touched that she trusted him enough to let him see her like this.

Eventually, he began to rub her shoulder, trying to ease her grief, and realized that he could hold her like this for the rest of his life.

Oh, God, no. Her reputation. And his grief, which he hadn't quite absorbed yet. He couldn't do this to her.

As Molly quieted, her tears no longing running, she felt comforted. No one in a long time had offered her the comfort Callum gave her right then. Sitting on his lap, being held so gently, awakened a whole different kind of need than the desire she had felt before. She wanted to burrow into the warmth and strength he offered her.

She wanted it never to end. Dangerous. But she let herself enjoy it, anyway. It would end soon enough. Reality would return, as it always did.

Regardless, she'd realized in those minutes that although she was surrounded by people, by friends, she nearly always felt alone in some deep corner of her heart.

But at last, she had to move. Had to resume her life. Had to stand up and be the pastor again. As if to remind her, the phone rang.

Hardly able to smother a sigh, she eased off Callum's lap and then hurried to answer the phone in her kitchen. At the other end, she heard Tyra's voice.

"Molly, I don't know where that damn detective is, but I suspect you do. Tell him that Vera Holmes saw someone lurking in the back alley. She called me, heaven knows why. Am I a ninja?"

Her first concern was for her friend, then for Vera. "Tyra, are you okay?"

"I'm fine," Tyra said, sounding almost angry. "But I'm not sure you're safe! Now get to it, girl!"

Molly hung up and turned around to find Callum standing right behind her.

"What?" he demanded, as if he suspected the news.

"Vera Holmes. She lives on the other side of the alley behind the church parking lot. She saw a lurker and Tyra wanted me to tell you."

Right then, she didn't even think of what it meant that Tyra wanted her to tell Callum. She didn't care that apparently everyone knew right where he was. All she cared about was Vera Holmes.

THE EMOTIONS ROILING in Arthur Killian were like a pressure cooker ready to blow. They'd driven him out on this cold night to hunt at the parsonage only to see that that damn woman wasn't alone again. She used to be alone at night all the time since he'd arrived here to stalk her, but now she was never alone.

He shouldn't have wasted time working out his needs on those other women while circling in on Molly, hoping to frighten her. He shouldn't have tried to play the distraction game. He should have just gone for Molly Canton's throat.

Not so smart after all, he told himself. Man, he was almost stupid, playing his foolish little game while the rabbit kept avoiding the snare.

Standing in the alley, staring at the lights in her house, having seen that damn detective show up with a paper bag, he hated that woman more than ever.

But she wasn't alone. She *had* to be alone. He was smart enough to know he couldn't take down more people than that woman with anything but a gun. But a gun wouldn't satisfy him. Wouldn't satisfy his urges. He needed to beat her until her blood ran over the floor.

The other women hadn't been the same. They'd been

stopgaps, nothing more. Only Molly Canton could satisfy him.

He clenched his fists inside his gloves and resisted
an urge to scream his fury.

Then he settled on the house right behind him. He
knew a woman lived there alone. When he'd been
picking out victims, he'd watched more than three.
Alone. And this one had a light on, and he enjoyed
seeing the blood spill. Until a dark shadow moved in
the corner of his vision.

He melted away into trees and shrubs and took a
roundabout route to his stolen car, knowing he was
leaving prints in the snow, but he quickly reached a
shoveled sidewalk. He crossed a street and melted into
more shrubbery alongside the walk. Three minutes
later he climbed into the car and drove away slowly.

Appearing to be just a local resident, not someone
in a hurry. Another smart move. Maybe he wasn't a
fool after all.

MOLLY WATCHED CALLUM swing into high gear, punching a button on his phone. Then he was speaking.

"Guy? You know Vera Holmes's house? Get some
men in plainclothes over there as fast as you can. A
man is standing in the alley between the church lot
and her. Right."

Then he started to yank on his outwear as fast as he
could. "Molly you stay here and lock the door. Prop a
chair under the latch so it's not easy to get in. Then pick

up the heaviest item you own and wait behind that door on the hinge side. Got it?"

Her fear, mostly for Vera, ramped up rapidly to nerve-stretching tension. "Got it."

Callum stopped just long enough to touch her arm. "Promise me."

"I promise. But get going."

She watched him slip out the door almost silently, then she did as he'd directed, all the while praying that Vera would be safe, that Callum wouldn't get hurt.

Then she picked up her fireplace poker. She doubted this creep had ever seen what military training taught a soldier to do with a rod. She sure as hell knew how to use it.

OUTSIDE, THE COLD air nearly snatched away Callum's breath. Moving as quietly as he could, keeping to the shadows, he slipped toward the alley, almost positive that this was their perp. He pushed down his throat-tightening fear for Molly to the furthest reaches of his mind. He needed every ounce of his focus on the minutes ahead.

He thought he saw a shadow move, blending into the night. Then hurrying feet came from his side.

He turned quickly, ready for anything, then recognized Guy Redwing, who spoke immediately, quietly. "I saw him slip into the shadows under the trees over there." He pointed.

"Ask Connie Parish to check on Vera Holmes. We can track this monster over the snow."

Guy tipped his head so that the radio microphone on

his shoulder was close to his mouth, allowing him to speak quietly.

Then he turned to Callum. "Connie is going to Vera's."

Callum nodded, thinking that at this point Vera would respond better to a woman's voice outside her house. Then he and Guy moved toward the place where the man had disappeared. As he'd hoped, there were footprints clear in the snow.

Guy adjusted his flashlight to a pinpoint to lead the way. No moon tonight to guide them. No moon to illuminate that dark figure if he slipped deeper under the trees. Enough light, thanks to the snow, to give a pale, silvery sheen to the ground, but not enough to distinguish figures in the deep shadows.

Callum, his heart beating a steady but strong rhythm, walked beside Guy, taking care not to mess up the footprints.

They reached the street and everything changed. No prints in the frozen patina over the street.

"He had to go somewhere," Guy said.

"Yeah, but which way?" Callum turned on his own flashlight, widened the beam and began to sweep the street and sidewalks for a clue. Then he thought he found one at the edge of the far sidewalk, right up close to bushes and the shadowing trees. Then more. They followed them as rapidly as they could, as the prints disappeared then reappeared farther on down.

Callum jerked his head up as he heard a car start. On the night air, it probably sounded closer than it was, so he guessed it was at least a block away. But the engine didn't rev—instead, it sounded as if it was driving away slowly.

Nonetheless, he felt it in his gut. He turned to Guy Redwing. "That's him. He got away."

Guy answered with a reluctant nod, then a string of curses. "We don't know which way he went. We could get some cars over there…"

"Too late," Callum answered. "He could hide that car almost anywhere there are other cars because we don't know the make, color or model. He could hunker down so we couldn't tell he's inside unless we want to shine flashlights into every car in a five-mile radius."

"That'd be a whole lot of cars," Guy said grimly.

"Yeah." Callum shook his head, a relatively mild response to what he was feeling: overwhelming frustration. "We need to talk to Vera Holmes, find out how much she saw."

It was going to be a long night. Or morning. They'd have to question neighbors, too, all along the alley, in the hope that someone besides Vera had noticed something.

Guy spoke again as they walked back to the rear of the church. "You go check on the Pastor, Cal. Then we'll talk to Vera."

Shock jolted Callum. He'd believed he and Molly were being relatively circumspect, and damn, they were only friends, anyway.

But apparently the Conard County grapevine was busy, probably with a very different interpretation. One that Molly had wanted to avoid. One that might harm her position.

He gave himself a mental kick for being so careless after she'd warned him.

Then he headed for the parsonage door. Molly deserved to know that for right now she and Vera were safe.

Molly waited beside the door, poker in hand, her heartbeat steady, her mood strangely calm. Adrenaline, she thought. Just adrenaline.

Her wait seemed to last an eternity before she heard a knock at the door, followed by Callum's voice. At once she pulled the bracing chair from beneath the latch and threw open the door.

Callum started to step in, then paused as he looked at her. "I figured some kind of candlestick or a cast-iron pan."

"What are you talking about?" Then she realized she was still holding the fireplace poker. "Oh."

"It's okay," he said, taking the poker from her and carrying it back to its stand. "He didn't have time to get to Vera, but she's probably pretty shaken. I need to go back to talk with her. But whoever was in that alley managed to escape, damn it."

Molly clapped her hand to her mouth, holding in her own instinctive string of curses. "Dang, Callum!"

"He caught sight of something. Maybe I didn't stick to the deep shadows well enough. Or maybe he glimpsed one of the deputies approaching. Whatever, he took off. We were able to track him at least part of the way but as near as I can tell, he took off in a car before we reached him."

"Oh, God. Oh, God."

Callum turned from the fireplace and wrapped her in his arms, holding her tightly against his still-cold jacket.

"I'm going to make you safe," he said tautly. "I promise."

"But what about other women?" she asked. "I can't stand that anyone else is suffering because of me. I can't stand it!"

He leaned back a bit and ran his gloved hand over her hair. "When we get him, everyone will be safe."

Then he let go of her. "I've got to go. This night isn't over." He paused. "I promised to make you safe, but I can't guarantee he won't find a way to swing around us and get back here. Keep that door locked and prop the chair against it. And stay close to that poker."

"And keep the lights off," she added shakily. "I will."

When Callum was gone, Molly stood alone in the cozy space that no longer felt cozy. Not in the least. She understood his promise, but she also understood that he couldn't guarantee anything.

Everything was too fluid. Knowing Killian's identity wouldn't make him easier to find if he was in flight. And he could always come back later. A week. A month. Unless he was captured, she wouldn't be the only woman at risk from that monster.

The idea sickened her that she could be the cause of so much pain. *No good deed goes unpunished.* A depressing thought and so far from her usual nature that it disturbed her. She couldn't let Killian change her. That would be worse than being beaten. It would mean she'd lost.

By nature she was a fighter, not a quitter, and she wasn't going to let that man steal his way into her mind.

After locking up, as Callum wanted, she went to the kitchen and made herself some sugar-free cocoa. Which probably had as many calories one way or another as the real stuff, but it felt better to her diet-conscious self.

With the poker near at hand, she settled into her rocker in the dark to wait out the endless night hours. Any desire to sleep must have moved to the next state because her eyelids didn't feel even a bit heavy. Another time her insomnia was useful. The heat kicked on, sounding loud in the night's quiet. The Christmas tree shimmered in the corner, full of a promise that seemed to be escaping her.

Arthur Killian had not only beaten three women badly, but he was also stealing the sense of safety from every single woman in this town.

And he was stealing Christmas from all of them.

She half wished she'd get the chance to use the poker on him.

CITY POLICE AND sheriff's deputies prowled the streets and alleys of Conard City even though they believed the search was useless. They *had* to try.

For a while, Callum sat with Connie Parish and Vera Holmes. Vera had wrapped herself in a colorful afghan and held a mug full of hot tea in both her hands.

"Did you get the sense that anyone might be watching you or your house before tonight?" Callum asked.

Vera shook her head. "Not once. But that's not the kind of thing you think about around here, even with those attacks. Maybe we all wander around believing it won't happen to us."

"So just tonight?" Callum asked.

"Just seeing a man in the alley at that time of night, that was the only thing. He was pacing a little, but not much, as if he was waiting for something." Her eyes lifted from her mug. "I couldn't really see much more. He was like a black shadow. If he hadn't moved, I might never have noticed him at all."

"How did you see him?" Callum asked. "Wouldn't light inside make it hard to see out there?"

Vera sighed. "I was a fool, I guess. I turned off the light in the kitchen as I always do when I go to bed. Automatic. I woke up to go to the bathroom, then wanted a glass of water, and since I know my way around this house so well, I didn't even turn the kitchen light on again to get the water. That's when I saw him."

Little enough, Callum thought when he departed. Connie offered to stay the rest of the night with Vera, and the woman accepted gratefully.

Then he was back out in the cold and the only thing he felt good about was that they'd scared the creep. But the scare wouldn't keep him away for long, because he hadn't gotten his prize.

Callum picked up his vehicle from the church parking lot and headed toward the office. In the morning, the door knocking would start, over a wider area than the alley because the guy had gone somewhere and someone might have seen something just that little bit unusual.

This was going to take just about all the manpower they could spare. Back in the office, he listened to the crackling communications between officers, sparse at this time of night.

He had to get a picture of this Arthur Killian out to the public. Sticking it on a few windows wouldn't be enough.

He wondered if the Conard County weekly paper, full of ads and little news, could deliver the mug shot the way they delivered the paper: to nearly every driveway. Man, that would be a lot of copies but the paper, like many, was printed out of town. How many copiers would he be able to access around here? The schools, local businesses, the library. He was sure everyone would want to help. He needed to get that rolling first thing in the morning.

But maybe he could get some assistance from nearby television stations. All he had to do was call, explain and ask.

That was when he realized he was tired despite all the activity. He was running in circles trying to figure out how to get Killian's photo and description out there and trying to mentally count copy machines. Damn. Just call a few TV stations and tell 'em what was going on. Simple. Quick.

A hell of a lot faster than trying to string together every copy machine in town. What in the world had he been thinking?

He remembered the cot in the conference room. Usually folded against a wall, but occasionally used by a deputy who needed a nap after a long shift when he had to get back on the street soon. Sooner than he could reach his own bed. Not all of them lived in or near town.

Maybe he could catch some shut-eye back there. The uniforms knew what they were doing. There was a dispatcher who'd wake him if he was needed.

But if he didn't catch some shut-eye he wouldn't be of any use at all.

MOLLY WAS STILL wide-awake when the first rosy light of dawn tried to peek around tiny cracks in her curtains. During the night she had grown chilled, so she headed for the kitchen to make some instant oatmeal.

The threat for this night was over. The daytime seemed to scare away that coward. Killian was certainly a coward, a man who beat up on people who were smaller than he was. Like his wife. And who knew how many others.

Like now, here in Conard City. Women, and women alone. Yeah, he was a coward, but feeling all tough inside his own mental delusion.

But what difference did that make? He was still hurting people. The kind of man he was or believed himself to be was irrelevant.

What she really needed was some plan to stop him.

Her cell phone rang just after she'd washed her oatmeal bowl and was drying her hands. Tyra. She answered quickly, glad to hear her friend's voice.

"I take it you're okay," Tyra said dryly. "The police presence back here has been astonishing. I never dreamed this small town had so many cops."

"You should take a head count."

Tyra laughed, a sound that was cut short. "Sorry, the damn ribs are still giving me a hard time. But not to worry. I'm healing. Just don't tell me any jokes."

"I doubt I could come up with a funny one right now. But at least Vera is all right."

"Yes, she is. Her guardian deputy, Connie Parish, I think, let me talk to her. What a change from when she first called me about the man in the alley. Right now she sounds ready to take him on. At least the bastard didn't try to get into her house. She wouldn't be feeling so feisty this morning."

No, he wanted to get into my house and couldn't because Callum was hanging around. Again, the thought sickened her, because what if Killian had decided to sate himself by going after Vera? What if he'd gotten inside?

"Molly? Where'd you go, girl?"

Molly realized she'd fallen silent. "Sorry. My insomnia again." She wasn't about to tell Tyra what she now knew about Killian. She didn't want Tyra worrying about her.

"I wish I could get back to school," Tyra said.

"Did the doctor tell you how long it would be?"

"I can't go back until I'm able to yell at the kids."

A surprised laugh escaped Molly. "You're kidding, right?"

"Of course, I'm kidding. Dang it, Molly, you *must* be sleepy. Anyway, Doc thinks another week. I won't be singing carols until then, I guess."

"I'm sorry."

"About what? That I won't be singing? The world will be grateful. Anyway, go find your pillow and catch some sleep, why don't you?"

"I've got a lot to do today."

"You always have a lot to do, and most of it can wait until you've had a few hours of sleep. I'm sure the inestimable Henrietta can hold the fort for a little while. Now scoot to bed or I'll come over there and sing at you."

Smiling, Molly said goodbye. Tyra was right. At last she was feeling sleepy. At last.

She wended her way to her bed, climbed into her pajamas and fell asleep almost as soon as her head touched the pillow.

ARTHUR KILLIAN WAS one furious man. Not only had he been thwarted last night and chased, but he also couldn't go back to that lousy motel room, where it was at least warm even if it did reek of ash. He'd spent most of the night curled up on the back seat under a blanket that stank of some kind of animal. Now he was freaking cold, sitting in a car he'd heisted, which would undoubtedly be reported, in a parking lot surrounded by other cars.

As daylight began to edge away the night with a

ruddy glow, he decided that he needed to get farther away for just a little while. Let the heat die down.

He bit into another peanut-butter cracker and took a swig from a beer. Hell, he should have gotten coffee at that convenience store. At least it would be hot.

But as he thought about heading for a larger town, just to let the heat die down a bit, he knew he couldn't.

Something bigger than himself was driving him and he couldn't shake it, not for even a little while. He craved teaching that woman a lesson as much as he craved the air he breathed.

So he'd get another car, preferably one that could put out more heat that this little one. He'd need gas soon, anyway, if he was going to run the damn things nonstop.

But even buying gas was becoming more dangerous. He wondered if they'd somehow found out who he was. Nah. Then *maybe*. But how? He'd been so damn careful.

He tossed the cracker. It didn't taste good with the beer. He should have gotten some kind of chips or nuts. Next time.

As he sat there, shivering, he tried not to remember his brilliant plan to cause a distraction so nobody'd ever guess that Molly Canton was his intended target.

Because now it looked like major stupidity.

Hell. He dumped the beer into the snow and headed back to the convenience store to get a couple of those giant mugs and fill them with coffee. He'd pick up a half dozen of those sweet rolls, too. At least they'd taste good with the coffee.

He didn't like the way the clerk looked at him, as if it was weird that he'd come back a second time.

Well, it was a free country, wasn't it?

Chapter Seventeen

Callum went to the parsonage that evening, unable to see any reason to avoid it. Near as he could tell, he and Molly had become an "item" in the minds of many people. If that caused her trouble, it was too late to fix it.

He was concerned about her reaction to recent events. He also wanted to be with her, but he told himself that was a minor thing compared to her state of mind, after how close that bastard had gotten to her.

Although he'd figured out she was a sturdy woman who could take a lot in her stride. So, okay, he mostly wanted to spend some time with her. Lying to himself rarely worked any better than people who tried to lie to him in an interrogation. But it was amazing how many stories people could invent. Stories that were as full of holes as Swiss cheese.

He stopped to eat beforehand so she wouldn't feel she needed to cook for him and could have one of her small frozen meals to appease her concern about weight.

He still didn't get it. She was a beautiful woman

just as she was, and she'd still be beautiful if she gained more weight. But while he might not understand it, she'd sure made it clear that he should keep his opinion on that subject to himself, that it was her decision.

Fair enough.

She greeted him with that warm smile he was coming to love. The way it softened her face, made her look so gentle and kind and welcoming. How well it fit her nature.

"Want some dinner?" she asked him as he started pulling off his outerwear.

"I ate already, thanks, so just take care of yourself, please."

She laughed lightly. "I already ate, too. But I do have a pot of coffee. Odd that I have insomnia sometimes, but the amount of caffeine I drink in the evening seems to have no bearing on it."

"The coffee sounds great."

They moved into the living room, where the tree twinkled and the fire glowed with embers. Callum stirred them a bit with a poker, then took another log out of the large wood box that filled a back corner of the room. It wasn't long before fire lapped at the sides of the log.

"So tell me," he said, "do you go out and chop this wood yourself? It wouldn't surprise me."

She laughed quietly. "I thought I'd told you that Jimmy, Marvin, and a couple of other men keep that box well-stocked. People take care of me, Callum."

He returned to the recliner, adjusting the pillow

before he sat. "Not well enough. They need to get you some new chairs, too."

"*You* talk to the wardens then. The church comes first."

"And you're part of that church. A very important part." He hesitated, then said, "You know people are talking. I shouldn't come here anymore."

"Oh, heck," she said irritably. "I'm not a cloistered nun. I'm entitled to a life and friends. If they can't take it, I'll move on."

"But you said…"

"I know what I said. Then I realized I've been tip-toeing too much because some people didn't like the idea of a woman pastor. Well, you know what? I finally got around to deciding that they *have* a woman pastor and they should be judging me on my performance in the job, not on my being female. It's independence day for me."

He had to laugh. "Good for you, Molly Canton."

"Well, it's true. It's not as if I'm getting drunk at the bar every night or swearing from the pulpit. Then they might have something to complain about."

He smiled at her because she always made him smile. He was coming out of his gloom at last. An odd feeling, one that brought a spark of guilt, but only a small one. He was getting past that, too.

And she was bringing him to this point. Her joy in life, her joy in the holiday season, had begun to thaw the ice that had encased him for so long.

And the desire he felt for her. A feeling he hadn't

allowed himself since Angela. He felt it now and he didn't feel the least bit guilty about that, either.

He couldn't deny himself any longer. Rising, he held a hand out to her. She looked perplexed but took his hand and stood up. Then she looked into his eyes and he knew she could see the fire burning there. Fires he needed to quench. He wondered if she felt the same, but then she leaned into him, wrapping her arms around his waist.

"Oh, Callum," she breathed. "Please."

He needed no further invitation. Sweeping her along with him to the bedroom, where the chill was greater, but ignorable, he lifted her sweater over her head, exposing her plain cotton bra. Then with a flick, he unfastened it and let it fall to the floor.

Her breasts fell free, revealing a surprise to him. She was not as small-breasted as she appeared when dressed. Another concession to her role?

She wasn't busty. No, her breasts were on the smaller side but perfect, tip-tilted with pink areolas and nipples. He circled her nipples with his thumbs, then kissed and sucked until she hardened. It didn't take long. She was coming along with him.

Her breaths quickened, quickening his body.

"Callum," she murmured. "Hurry up. It's chilly."

He almost laughed with pleasure, but he listened to her. Stripping her clothes away, he found more perfect delights. She was rounded, but it was womanly rounding, the kind that looked soft and had all the right curves.

"Get under the blanket," he said roughly. "Get warm while I get cold."

A happy but husky laugh escaped her as she slipped into the bed, devouring him with her eyes as he tossed his own clothing aside.

"You're gorgeous," she said quietly. "Gorgeous."

"Debatable." But he was glad she thought so. Then he slipped under the covers with her, drawing her heat toward him.

HE *WAS* GORGEOUS, she thought. Rangy and with lean muscles, as if he must run a lot, or walk a lot. A kind of muscling she liked.

But then, she was pressed against him while he stroked her and kissed her all over. She reciprocated as best she could, savoring the feel of his skin against her palms.

Perfect. Her insides throbbed so hard they almost hurt. He drove her wild, touching her most private places as if they had been made for him.

Then he slipped inside her, filling a space that had been empty for too long.

She felt as if she stopped breathing during those moments. Afterward she didn't remember breathing again until a cry of nearly painful pleasure escaped her.

He tumbled into completion with her.

TWO SWEATY BODIES wrapped in their own heat while winter lurked outside.

"Heaven," Molly murmured.

"Heaven can't hold a candle to this."

"Maybe not." She gave a soft laugh.

Then the parsonage phone rang in her little office across the hall.

"Ignore it," he suggested.

"I can't. People need help any hour of the day, even late at night. Or just someone to talk to."

She could feel his reluctance as he let her go. Unwrapping herself from him was painful, but the phone continued to ring.

Grabbing her bathrobe, ignoring her bare feet on the icy floor, she ran to grab the receiver.

"Hello, Pastor," said a man.

"Hello," she replied, trying to place that voice. It tickled the edge of her memory. "Can I help you?"

"Remember me? I'm coming for you," the voice said. "I'm coming for you and you won't live to regret it."

Then a slam and the line went dead.

She stood holding the receiver. Now she remembered the voice. The chill had begun to reach her heart.

"Molly?" Callum came into the office. "Molly? Do you need to go out?"

Slowly she hung up the phone. Her hand trembled and she felt ashamed of it.

"Molly?"

"That was Arthur Killian. He said he's coming for me."

Chapter Eighteen

It wasn't long before Molly showed her stubborn streak and became as immovable as the western mountains.

She refused to let Callum tell any of his colleagues. "They'll just scare him away."

"That's good."

She shook her head. "Not if he goes after another woman. I cannot and will not be responsible for that. Do you hear me, Callum? I won't. I'd rather be beaten to a pulp."

He winced, his fists clenching and unclenching. "I can't allow that."

"You're going to have to. Because if you try to stop him to protect me, his future victims will be on your head. I know you wouldn't be able to bear that any more than I could."

He wished he could deny it, but she was right about that. Even if he protected Molly, he'd wind up hating himself if another woman was hurt.

He spread his hands, frustrated to the point of explo-sion. "So what are you going to do? Expose yourself to that bastard? Take that risk? How much do you think I'll be able to stand *that*?"

"It's *my* decision."

"You can't stop me from being a cop."

"Maybe not. But you've got other people to worry about, too. They count at least as much. He's not going to come for me when I'm not alone."

"How in the hell do you know that?"

"Because the man is a coward through and through. He might beat up on women who are alone, but he won't take the risk when she's not alone. Weaker, smaller, defenseless. That's what he wants. Well, he won't find me defenseless."

Callum stifled his anger, his fear for her. He had to handle this calmly. "Your National Guard training, right? That's what you're going to rely on?"

She nodded.

"Damn it, Molly that was years ago. You're rusty."

She tipped up one corner of her mouth. "Ever heard of muscle memory? It's like riding a bike."

"Riding a bike?" he repeated in disbelief.

"Yes," she said firmly. "Like riding a bike. When I picked up that poker I felt the muscle memory kick in. He's lucky he didn't come through that door, because my body knew exactly what to do with him, and that poker felt right in my hands. Now leave it, Callum."

"How am I supposed to leave it? I give a great big damn about you, Molly."

"Then go back to your office and do *your* thing. You can come to the curtain call."

The curtain call? She was serious. Deadly serious.

"I told you once not to interfere with my decisions, Callum. That includes right now."

Her damn independence. Problem was, if he honored it, this time she could get seriously hurt or dead. But if he didn't honor it, Molly might turn her back on him forever.

Damned if he did, damned if he didn't.

Her voice grew quieter even as it remained firm. "You have to catch him before you can protect everyone. Trust me, I'll catch him for you."

He departed, as she'd demanded. But he was sure of one thing: Molly might appear to be alone, but he was going to make damn sure she wasn't. He'd wait outside in concealment every single night to make sure she wasn't.

Setting herself up as bait. For Pete's sake! All he could do was grind his teeth.

IT WAS THREE more days before Killian came for her. Three days in which she followed her normal routine. Choir rehearsals. Gathering more gifts for disadvantaged children and helping to wrap them. Keeping a friendly eye on the committee that was planning the Christmas dinner and getting volunteers from cooks to servers to cleanup. Asking local groceries for even more food, most of it willingly donated.

Visiting the homebound, like Stacy Withers, who was still feeling guilty about her terminal breast cancer and leaving her children behind. Like Marcia

Lathrop, who was caring for the curmudgeonly father of hers who had the beginnings of Alzheimer's. So many people, so many problems, and she could do little except provide a kind ear, or try to rustle up a volunteer to help ease their burdens.

But every night she felt eyes on her as she walked alone to the pastorage. She might be imagining it but she feared she was not.

Once inside, she followed her usual routine, making a frozen dinner, going to her office to finish some routine paperwork, and work on next Sunday's sermon. The fourth Sunday in Advent. Christmas peeking right around the corner now.

Around ten, she turned the rocker to face the door and put the poker beside it. Then she turned on all the downstairs lights and waited. She knew that Killian could see the light escaping even through the insulated curtains.

Her nerves stretched as the hours passed, but only a bit. She very much wanted to hit Killian a couple of times with that poker, maybe even get him in the family jewels again.

Not the kind of thoughts a pastor who taught forgiveness and turning the other cheek should have.

But she had them, anyway.

Not hers to judge? Killian deserved every bit of judgment this world could heap on him.

She was going to have to pray a whole lot for her own forgiveness, but she didn't care. Not right now. This man needed to be stopped.

It was on the third night two days after the third Sunday in Advent that her moment came.

CALLUM HAD MANAGED to secret himself in the shadow of one of the church's buttresses, facing Molly's cottage. He wore all black, his face as covered as the rest of him.

It was damn cold, but he didn't care if he turned into an icicle because he wasn't going to let Molly face this alone, whatever she wanted.

She'd get her licks in before he could reach her door. That ought to satisfy her. But then he'd be there to ensure she could take down Killian rather than lose the battle.

Too bad if she despised him for it, but nothing would make him allow her to face this threat alone. Nothing.

Each night, he'd watched her turn on lights and leave them on throughout the small house. She was waiting inside, waiting for a monster who wanted to hurt her savagely, even kill her. Waiting in the light for her hunter.

She probably wasn't sleeping at all, either. Nerves stretched as tightly as his.

He wished he could have persuaded her not to do this, but short of locking her in a holding cell, there was nothing. He admired her determination, understood her reasoning about more people getting hurt.

But he sure as hell didn't like it.

That pastor had a will of steel. He wondered if her congregation had any idea. Probably not. They'd probably never seen it and many most likely saw her in stereotypical terms. Her authority with them resided in her collar. It ought to reside in *her*.

And to think she'd been battling those attitudes since she arrived here. From what he could tell, she'd made significant headway, but he was willing to bet that none of those people had sensed her stubbornness and determination. Had realized that she hadn't left only because she didn't quit.

Now this. He wanted to get his hands around Arthur Killian's throat. He was used to this stuff, had learned to distance himself in order to keep his own mind clear and his life from going off the edge.

But with Molly, all that distance had vanished. She'd worked her way into his heart. What that meant he wasn't sure—he just knew there'd be a gaping hole inside him if anything happened to her.

God, for a hot cup of coffee. Something to warm him from the inside because the cold was sure stealing heat from his outside, even with the new thermal underwear he'd bought, even with felt-lined boots. He needed to move to stay warm, but he had to be very careful not to make noise, not to move enough that his shadow stood out among shadows.

Frostbite, here we come.

Then his eyes, well adapted to the dark by 2:00 a.m, caught sight of a movement just at the rear corner of the parsonage. Adrenaline slammed into him, pushing his heart to a fast beat. It flooded his limbs and made it extremely difficult to hold still.

No choice yet. No choice. As every muscle in his body coiled, he waited for the right moment. He had to get the guy *after* he broke in, when it could be proven that he was the perp by more than fingerprints alone. He'd had enough experience in court to know that just fingerprints couldn't bring about a conviction. One partial at one scene could have come from an ordinary visit. The prints he'd picked up at the diner were nearly useless because they didn't link Killian to any crime. They were good enough only to identify a possible perp. *Possible perp.* Enough for a defense lawyer to shred the case.

The dark figure moved again, slipping to Molly's door. Just another minute or two.

MOLLY HEARD THE fumbling at the latch. *Killian.* She picked up the poker and waited with it in her right hand hanging over the arm of the rocker. Out of sight. He wouldn't know.

Which was just what he wanted. Let him come in here and threaten her, take a swing at her. He'd live to regret it.

The door creaked open and she saw him as he hurried in and closed it behind him. All in black, head to foot.

"Well, well, Molly Canton," said a rough voice that could still cause anger to slither down her spine. "You're mine now."

"What the hell are you doing, Arthur? This could get you into trouble."

"You stole my wife from me. You hid her so well I can't find her to teach her a lesson." He pulled off his mask and scowled at her. "You sent me to prison. Now it's my turn to send you to hell."

He was still a tall fireplug of a man, too much beer showing on his belly. He had a shaved head that was an attempt to conceal his baldness and made up for that baldness with a scraggly beard. He reeked.

His fists were made for punching, though.

Molly tilted her head a bit, gauging the distance between them. "I think you've got that wrong, Arthur. If either of us goes to hell, it'll be you."

"I'm not talking about some fairy tale of an afterlife, Molly. I'm talking about the here and now. I'm going to rearrange your face. I'm going to kick you until you can't breathe. I've been debating whether to kill you, but I sure as hell want to see your blood all over the floor. I want to make sure you never forget what you did to me."

He was stepping closer, his hands clenching and unclenching. His bulky body leaning forward to give him the chance to swing a fist at her. Tough guy.

"What?" he asked. "Not going to try to defend yourself? Where's your fight?"

"You like women to fight back, do you?"

"A little feistiness makes it more fun, don't you think? At least you'll give yourself some stupid idea that you tried to save yourself. But there's no saving yourself now."

He raised his arm and she saw the punch coming toward the side of her head. She didn't even rise from the rocker as she swung the poker around and slammed his arm before his fist could reach her.

At once he cried out, punch forgotten.

Molly rose, still holding the poker. "How many more of your bones do you want me to break, Arthur? Maybe as many as you broke of your wife's bones? Maybe as many as you broke on the women around here? That could wind up being every single bone in your body."

She raised the poker again and watched Arthur cower backward with his good arm raised in front of his face. "I always knew you were a coward, Arthur. Now if you don't want me to swing again, get face-down on the floor."

Before he could comply, the door burst open and Callum barged in. In an instant he grabbed Killian's hands behind him and pulled out a zip cuff from his pocket. Killian yowled the whole time about his arm.

"You okay?" he asked Molly.

"It's him you should worry about. His arm is bro-ken." Then quietly she added, "Callum, thank you."

He looked up from Arthur. "For what?"

"For waiting out there in spite of what I said. For saving me from beating him to death."

Then she turned her back on the scene, sickened by that man, and sickened by her own act of violence. Sickened by the seething urges she'd felt to keep on hurting Arthur Killian.

She had wanted to beat him to a pulp.

Chapter Nineteen

The Fourth Sunday in Advent. The lighting of the last purple candle in the Advent wreath. A full church, this time full of gratitude that women were finally safe from Killian.

The singing from the congregation sounded brighter, more voices joining in with the choir. "O Come, O Come, Emmanuel" felt as if it held extra significance this year.

Joy had returned to Molly. Her pleasure in the beauty and hope of the season filled her, restoring her. Christmas would not be stolen this year, not from anyone.

The church basement brimmed with wrapped presents for the less fortunate children. The Christmas meal planning was done, the volunteers in line. At her suggestion, families had begun to adopt "grandparents," the elderly who would be alone, and bring them into their homes for the holiday. Some of those "grandparents" would become long-term friends.

Molly couldn't have asked for more. The smiles

she shared with people in the narthex as they left were broader than usual, warmer than ever. Her heart swelled.

As the crowd thinned, Callum came to stand beside her. She smiled at him then resumed talking to her congregants. When the last were gone, and as the Women's Club along with the Altar Society began a quick cleaning, he spoke.

"It appears that the gossip hasn't damaged your reputation any."

"No, it doesn't seem to have."

"Good. When you're done here, can I meet you at the parsonage?"

"Of course." She was well past the point of worrying about it. She wanted to see Callum and that was the beginning and end of it.

As he walked away, she felt his absence like an empty hole inside her. How was she ever to stand this when he finally told her he was still grieving? That pain had left little room in his heart.

Yes, he wasn't as grim as he'd been when she first met him and her wish to share some of the joy of this time of year had worked, at least in part.

But he was still a man who had lost a woman he'd loved with his whole heart.

Sighing, she went to remove her robes, then headed to the parsonage in her black uniform of collar and slacks, with thermal underwear in deference to the winter. Her red parka hung open, hardly needed in the short distance.

Callum was inside waiting for her, smiling. He'd turned on the Christmas tree, much to her surprise, and had built a fire on the hearth. He'd even made a pot of coffee, the aroma reaching her, as did the scent of the fire. Cheerful, warm, cozy.

"Are you done for the day?" he asked.

"Pretty much. A few phone calls I should make later, but they're not urgent."

"Then maybe you should get comfortable. That collar must be annoying."

She shook her head. "I got used to it. Anyway, I'm proud of it."

"You should be. But go get comfortable, anyway. Something warm, of course."

She changed into her sweats and her silly fuzzy slippers, then met him in the kitchen for coffee. As they had so often, they faced each other across the table, which now felt like a gulf between them. For fear of what might show in her eyes, she kept her gaze down, even though she wanted to stare at him, at the face she'd become so fond of.

Callum cleared his throat. "I was wondering…"

"Yes?"

"Would you be willing to risk your reputation even more by dating me?"

Her heart slammed and at last she looked at him. "Of course."

A smile began to dawn on his face. "That's a good start. But there's more."

"More?" She couldn't imagine.

"Molly Canton, I have come to love you very much and I'd like to make an honest woman of you. You know, to keep your congregants happy and protect your reputation."

A laugh spilled out of her. "To keep *them* happy? What about *me*?"

His smile broadened, but he looked oddly nervous. "Well, that's what I was easing my way into."

Molly felt her jaw drop.

"Callum?" she whispered.

"I told you I love you. Heart and soul. But I want more than friendship and dating. I want you for the rest of my life. I want us to marry."

"Oh, Callum." But a dam inside her broke and her heart filled with the love she felt for him. So fast, so sure, so true.

Unfortunately, he was beginning to look as if he believed she would refuse him.

But she couldn't, not for anything in this world. This was turning into her best Christmas ever.

"I love you," she said, her voice strengthening. "I love you and I definitely want to marry you."

A happy laugh escaped him. "Then what are we doing with this table between us?"

* * * * *

*Don't miss the other romances in Rachel Lee's
thrilling Conard County: The Next Generation
series:*

Conard County: Mistaken Identity
Conard County: Christmas Bodyguard
Conard County: Traces of Murder
Conard County: Hard Proof
Conard County Justice

Available now from Harlequin Books

 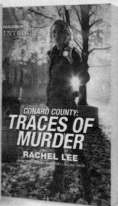

COMING NEXT MONTH FROM

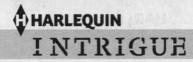

#2109 CHRISTMAS RANSOM

A Colt Brothers Investigation • by B.J. Daniels

Former rodeo star Davy Colt traded his competition spurs for a PI license. But even after years away, he never stopped loving hometown sweetheart Carla Richmond. When a robbery and hostage situation at the Lonesome bank leaves the loan officer injured and shattered, Davy will ransom his heart to avert a deadly Christmas for Carla.

#2110 CANYON KIDNAPPING

Eagle Mountain Search and Rescue • by Cindi Myers

Haunted by tragedy, Search and Rescue volunteer Sheri Stevens is determined to help find a missing child. Erik Lester, lead detective—and Sheri's ex-husband—is also dedicated to bringing the little girl home. As reigniting passion forges an even deeper bond between them, is this their second chance to vanquish the ghosts of the past?

#2111 DECODING THE TRUTH

Kansas City Crime Lab • by Julie Miller

A vicious hacker has KCPD lab tech Chelsea O'Brien dead in his sights, and Robert "Buck" Buckner won't let his personal heartbreak prevent him from keeping her safe. But the sparks between this reserved ex-cop and the warmhearted Chelsea are as hot as the trail they're tracking.

#2112 LOST IN LITTLE HAVANA

South Beach Security • by Caridad Piñeiro

Detective Roni Lopez has been keeping a secret from Detective Trey Gonzalez her whole life. When his partner is gunned down, she has a new secret to keep. But with their lives on the line, she has to make some tough choices about what really matters...

#2113 WYOMING CHRISTMAS STALKER

Cowboy State Lawmen • by Juno Rushdan

After Grace Clark witnesses a brutal murder, she tumbles headlong into a world of motorcycle gangs, cults and a young girl's secrets. Chief deputy sheriff Holden Powell's determined to discover what's wreaking havoc on their town this Christmas. He has something to prove, and he won't let anything happen to Grace—not on his watch.

#2114 BACKCOUNTRY COVER-UP

by Denise N. Wheatley

When her body is found on a hiking trail, deputy sheriff Todd Jacobson believes his sister was murdered. Her best friend, private investigator Elle Scott, agrees to help Todd prove it. Before long, Todd realizes he's Elle's only hope against becoming a corpse under the tree this Christmas.

YOU CAN FIND MORE INFORMATION ON UPCOMING HARLEQUIN TITLES, FREE EXCERPTS AND MORE AT HARLEQUIN.COM.

HICNM1022

The whole desperate plan began simply as a last-ditch attempt to save his life. He never intended for anyone to get hurt. That day, not long after Thanksgiving, he walked into the bank full of hope. It was the first time he'd ever asked for a loan. It was also the first time he'd ever seen executive loan officer Carla Richmond.

When he tapped at her open doorway, she looked up from that big desk of hers. He thought she was too young and pretty with her big blue eyes and all that curly chestnut-brown hair to make the decision as to whether he lived or died.

She had a great smile as she got to her feet to offer him a seat.

He felt so out of place in her plush office that he stood in the doorway nervously kneading the brim of his worn baseball cap for a moment before stepping in. As he did, her blue-eyed gaze took in his ill-fitting clothing hanging on his rangy body, his bad haircut, his large, weathered hands.

He told himself that she'd already made up her mind before he even sat down. She didn't give men like him a second look—let alone money. Like his father always said, bankers never gave dough to poor people who actually needed it. They just helped their rich friends.

Right away Carla Richmond made him feel small with her questions about his employment record, what he had for collateral, why he needed the money and how he planned to repay it. He'd recently lost one crappy job and was in the process of starting another temporary one, and all he had to show for the years he'd worked hard labor since high school was an old pickup and a pile of bills.

He took the forms she handed him and thanked her, knowing he wasn't going to bother filling them in. On the way out of her office, he balled them up and dropped them in the trash. All the way to his pickup, he mentally kicked himself for being such a fool. What had he expected?

HIEXP0922

No one was going to give him money, even to save his life—especially some woman in a suit behind a big desk in an air-conditioned office. It didn't matter that she didn't have a clue how desperate he really was. All she'd seen when she'd looked at him was a loser. To think that he'd bought a new pair of jeans with the last of his cash and borrowed a too-large button-up shirt from a former coworker for this meeting.

After climbing into his truck, he sat for a moment, too scared and sick at heart to start the engine. The worst part was the thought of going home and telling Jesse. The way his luck was going, she would walk out on him. Not that he could blame her, since his gambling had gotten them into this mess.

He thought about blowing off work, since his new job was only temporary anyway, and going straight to the bar. Then he reminded himself that he'd spent the last of his money on the jeans. He couldn't even afford a beer. His own fault, he reminded himself. He'd only made things worse when he'd gone to a loan shark for cash and then stupidly gambled the money, thinking he could make back what he owed and then some when he won. He'd been so sure his luck had changed for the better when he'd met Jesse.

Last time the two thugs had come to collect the interest on the loan, they'd left him bleeding in the dirt outside his rented house. They would be back any day.

With a curse, he started the pickup. A cloud of exhaust blew out the back as he headed home to face Jesse with the bad news. Asking for a loan had been a long shot, but still he couldn't help thinking about the disappointment he'd see in her eyes when he told her. They'd planned to go out tonight for an expensive dinner with the loan money to celebrate.

As he drove home, his humiliation began to fester like a sore that just wouldn't heal. Had he known even then how this was going to end? Or was he still telling himself he was just a nice guy who'd made some mistakes, had some bad luck and gotten involved with the wrong people?

Don't miss
Christmas Ransom *by B.J. Daniels,*
available December 2022 wherever
Harlequin books and ebooks are sold.

Harlequin.com

Get 4 FREE REWARDS!

We'll send you 2 FREE Books plus 2 FREE Mystery Gifts.

FREE Value Over **$20**

Both the **Harlequin Intrigue®** and **Harlequin® Romantic Suspense** series feature compelling novels filled with heart-racing action-packed romance that will keep you on the edge of your seat.

HARLEQUIN
PLUS

Announcing a **BRAND-NEW** multimedia subscription service for romance fans like you!

Read, Watch and Play.

Experience the easiest way to get the romance content you crave.

Start your **FREE 7 DAY TRIAL** at www.harlequinplus.com/freetrial.

Love Harlequin romance?

DISCOVER.

Be the first to find out about promotions,
news and exclusive content!

Facebook.com/HarlequinBooks

Twitter.com/HarlequinBooks

Instagram.com/HarlequinBooks

Pinterest.com/HarlequinBooks

You Tube YouTube.com/HarlequinBooks

ReaderService.com

EXPLORE.

Sign up for the Harlequin e-newsletter and
download a free book from any series at
TryHarlequin.com

CONNECT.

Join our Harlequin community to
share your thoughts and connect
with other romance readers!
Facebook.com/groups/HarlequinConnection